MOLLY AND COMPANY

MOLLY
AND
COMPANY

MARGARET A. WESTLIE

Selkirk
STORIES

ISBN 13: 978-0-9937344-2-7

Selkirk Stories™ and the image of a heart with three stars are trademarks of Selkirk Stories, Cornwall, Prince Edward Island, Canada.

Cover Design by A. Michael Shumate

Printed by CreateSpace, an Amazon.com Company

CHAPTER ONE

Gertrude Harvey yawned and stretched her slender body. The smell of coffee had awakened her. Mm, she thought sleepily, Don's up before me again. She lay still for a few more minutes savouring the luxury of being able to sleep as late as she wanted to. There was little traffic in this very old part of Charlottetown so nothing had disturbed her all night. The house, her childhood home, was solidly built and muted what little ambient noise there was.

"Up and at it, sleepy!" called Don from downstairs. "The day's a-wasting."

She stretched again and then rolled to a sitting position on the side of the bed, fishing for her slippers with her bare toes. What time is it, anyway? she wondered, peering at the bedside clock. Only nine yet, not bad for a Saturday. She came fully awake. *We're going out to Jim's this evening. It'll be nice. It's the first time since we were married.* She wandered off to the bathroom. A few minutes later she joined her husband of three weeks in the kitchen. "What's for breakfast?"

"Coffee and French toast," said Don. His large, athletic person was clad in a cable knit sweater. His nondescript brown hair and the sheep white of his sweater gave him a rather beige appearance.

"Mm, my favourite. I do love being taken care of."

"Everything's your favourite, and I do like taking care of you." He turned back to the task of cracking eggs. "The paper's there if you want to read it." He wiped the residue of raw egg from his fingers on Gertrude's flowered apron that covered his attire.

Gertrude settled herself at the heavy oak table with its square of embroidered cloth in the centre, picked up the Guardian and read the back page first. "Did you see this article? William Poste fell down the stairs at his home and sustained head injuries. He's in critical condition in the Neuro I.C.U."

"Yeah, it's too bad. I guess it happened while we were idling our time away in post-wedding bliss. That's just an update on his condition."

"I wonder what his wife'll do if he dies? She's pretty young, I heard."

"She'll have all his money. He's quite rich. His paintings have been fetching very large sums in the art markets. He's a legend in his own time, so they say." Don whipped the eggs one last time before dropping the bread into them.

Gertrude laughed. "Maybe she pushed him. Rumour has it that he wasn't very good to her."

"I don't know about that. She was always well dressed, the few times that I saw her. She didn't seem to lack for anything. She's a skinny little thing. She looks about thirteen playing dress-up." He dropped the dripping bread into the frying pan where it hissed and sputtered. "Just right," muttered Don to himself a few moments later as he turned each piece to the other side.

"Well there's more to being a good husband than just providing her with all the physical comforts."

"That's true," said Don. He slid a spatula under the toast and transferred it to a warmed plate. "Take you, for instance. If I recall, your dearest wish in life was to be able to cuddle anytime you wanted to." He nuzzled her neck as he passed her plate. "Are you getting enough cuddling these days, my dear?"

"Almost." Gertrude arched her neck for more attention.

"Almost! Almost! I'll have to hire a stand-in to provide you with any more than this," said Don.

"Who would you get?"

"Eat your breakfast," said Don.

It was good to see Jim again. He was a ghost hunter employed by the Psychical Research Institute as a free lancer. His dog, Betsy, who so much resembled her master in girth and general colouring, greeted them, her shaggy tail beating rapidly back and forth in her joy. She woofed and pranced about their feet in the yard on muddy paws, barely able to contain herself. "Stay down, Betsy," shouted Jim. His sturdy frame, clad in a brown sweater with white trim, filled the doorway. He stood aside. "Come on in folks, supper's ready as soon as Mary Ann gets here."

They entered the cozy old kitchen and hung their jackets in the accustomed place on the hooks behind the stove. The fire crackled cheerily in the cast iron stove, casting a warm glow over the entire room. The red and white table cloth, forever askew, covered the old-fashioned table between the windows. The red curtains had faded somewhat since the first time Gertrude had seen them and the pink geranium had succumbed to unintentional neglect and been replaced with a white one. On the mantel shelf, the grandmother clock still ticked noisily at every swing of its pendulum and wheezed into life to chime the hour and the half hour.

"It feels like home here," said Gertrude. She claimed the rocking chair. "What's keeping Mary Ann?"

"Oh, you know her, like the little dog's tail, always behind," said Jim. He stirred the gravy.

"Here she comes now," said Don. Head lights swept the dusk in the yard. A minute later Mary Ann entered. "Am I late?" As usual her greying brown hair was in disarray. She rarely had time to comb it properly or thought much about it after the initial tidying of the day.

"Not very," said Jim. "We were just going to send a search party."

Mary Ann giggled, her plump cheeks rose and almost covered her eyes. "The cat had her kittens in my bed this morning. I forgot to make it, you know. I couldn't get her to move them. I fixed up a very nice bed for them behind the stove but she just picked them right up and carried them back to mine. I don't know where I'll sleep tonight, they're still there."

"You'll think of something," said Jim. "Sit in everyone, supper's ready."

Chairs scraped as everyone found their usual places. "It's sure nice to have you guys back," said Mary Ann. "This place is dull without you now. Did you have a good time?" Her eyes twinkled. "You found everything all right?"

Gertrude blushed, unable to say a word.

"Mary Ann!" chided Jim. "Enough of that! You sound just like Molly."

"Speaking of Molly," said Don, "have you talked to her since she passed on?"

"No, I haven't," said Mary Ann. "I don't know what's happened to her in the last few weeks. I haven't even heard from Lucy. Maybe I should try to contact them after supper, since they haven't tried to contact me."

"That might be fun," said Gertrude. "I haven't done any trance work since the last time we were here, so I haven't heard from them either."

"Eat up," said Jim, "after supper is time enough to discuss Molly and Lucy. Pass the potatoes, Don."

"This sure is good chicken, what did you do to it?" Gertrude helped herself to a second piece.

"It's not chicken," said Jim. "It's rabbit. My friend that brought the deer meat last fall came by this morning with a pair already cleaned for me."

"Oh!" said Gertrude. "Bunnies."

"Not 'bunnies.' Wild rabbits that get into farmers' gardens and eat the profits and proliferate like crazy."

"I'll have to pretend it's chicken for now," said Gertrude. "Pass the gravy, please."

Supper continued with the sound of cutlery on china, accompanied by the cheerful snapping of the wood stove. The serving dishes made one last round. At last Jim said, "So what did you bring for dessert, Mary Ann?"

"I made an apple raisin pie. I thought we might have it warm with some ice cream, if you have any."

"I sure do. It's French vanilla. Will that suit?"

"Perfectly." Mary Ann began to cut the pie.

"I'll make coffee while I'm up, too," said Jim.

Molly MacIntosh yawned and stretched luxuriously. "That's the best sleep I've had in months," she thought. She opened her eyes to the sunlit room, not quite recognizing where she was. Everything felt different this morning. She looked at her arms and hands still stretched above her head, startled to see them young and unwrinkled, like they used to be. Indeed, they felt limber and supple like a young girl's. She pulled them down and inspected them closely, realizing as she did so that she didn't need to squint her eyes to bring them into focus.

"What's happened to me?" she thought in wonderment. She swung her legs lithely over the edge of the bed. "Where am I? This isn't my room at the nursing home!"

She began shouting in sudden panic. "NURSE! NURSE! HELP! HELP! Oh, why doesn't someone come?!"

The door opened with a tinkle of cutlery and glass, and her old friend Lucy's smiling face appeared.

"You're finally awake!" said Lucy. She set the tray on the bedside stand. "Have you had a good sleep?"

"Best sleep I've had in ages," said Molly. "Is that breakfast?"

"Yes, I thought you might like to have a real one your first day here, so I manifested it for you."

"Manifested?! Where am I? I thought you were dead!"

Lucy smiled sweetly. "Don't you remember? You've come over too."

Molly thought about this for a moment. "D'you mean I'm dead too?"

"That's right. You came over three weeks ago. You've been asleep ever since."

"Oh, yes." Molly suddenly remembered. "The therapeutic sleep." She began buttering her toast. "Is this the last breakfast I'll have?"

"It's the last one you'll need," replied Lucy. "You may want to continue the custom for a while. Some spirits do."

"Nice room." Molly looked around herself as she munched a bite of toast and egg. "Kind of like my room at Sunset Manor, only newer."

"Not bad for a rest home," said Lucy. "They try to make the surroundings you wake up in as much like what you're used to as possible, that way you won't be scared if you wake up unattended. This one's called Sunrise Manor."

Molly remembered the nursing home on Prince Edward Island where she had spent her last mortal days. The place had been old, its dark hallways and tiny rooms had seemed jail-like. At least it was clean, she thought to herself, and they did make an effort to brighten it up with paint and posters. The care was pretty good too, considering the conditions and the pay. She sopped up the last of her egg yolk with her last bite of bread.

"Have you seen Gertrude lately?" She took a sip of coffee. "Or Larry? Does he wear the capes and the Gainsborough hat with the big red feather here? Is he really our boss and is he just as bossy here as he was in the physical?"

Lucy straightened her cardigan and ran her fingers through her short brown hair. "To answer your questions in reverse order, yes Larry is still the same, still our boss and just as flamboyant and bossy. I haven't bothered Gertrude and Don these last few weeks, after all, they are just newlyweds. I thought they'd like some time to themselves, and Gertrude'll be working with Jim in his ghost hunting business, so we'll be seeing plenty of them later. Larry'll be by this morning sometime."

Molly looked again at her wrinkle-free hands and arms, and wondered aloud, "Is the rest of me like this?"

"Like what?"

"You know. Young-looking. Sort of smooth and fine again, like I was when I was a young woman."

"Yes, that was partly what all the sleeping was about."

Molly began patting herself everywhere, finally running her fingers through her hair, expecting to find the thin white wisps that had covered only parts of her scalp a few weeks ago. "I have hair again!" She almost shouted in her delight.

Lucy laughed at her friend's exuberance. "Of course you have hair, you silly thing. You're completely renewed."

"I'm not silly," scowled Molly. "I looked pretty awful a few weeks ago. No teeth and just a hair here and there." She suddenly realized she had teeth again too, and clicked them together joyously. She jumped off the bed and began searching the room frantically.

"What's the matter?" asked Lucy in some alarm.

"Where's there a mirror? I want to see myself."

"There's a long mirror in the lobby. You're allowed to look in it for ten seconds before you go out just to check your attire. They don't encourage vanity around here."

"Humph!" said Molly. "I can see that they don't. Ten seconds indeed! What have I got to wear anyway? You know how fussy I am, and the more drapery the better."

Lucy laughed at her again. "You'll get used to the limited viewing time. In the meantime, all you have to do is think about what you want to wear and it will manifest itself."

"Hm," replied Molly, "I think I'd like to wear my old blue caftan and that diamanté turban. Are they renewed too?"

"Everything is renewed here. You create it all again each time you think about it."

"In that case, I think I'll create a large diamond ring for my right hand, and a large sapphire ring for my left hand." She thought for a moment. "Perhaps some large drop earrings to complement the diamanté turban too, don't you think so, Lucy?"

Dessert had been consumed and coffee handed around when Jim said, "I have an announcement to make. If Gertrude is ready to come to work for me, I have a job to do."

Gertrude felt her skin prickle with excitement. "A ghost hunt?" Her eyes widened.

"Sort of," replied Jim. "Have you two been reading the papers lately, or have you been too busy?"

"We read this morning's paper," said Don. "What about it?"

"Did you see the little article on the back page updating Willie Poste's condition?"

"We sure did," said Gertrude. "What's the story on him anyway?"

"Apparently he fell down the stairs from his studio and cracked his skull on the newel post at the bottom," said Jim. "He's been in a coma ever since. I guess he has a severely depressed skull fracture. They're still hoping that he'll regain consciousness."

"That must've been quite a fall. His house is a lot like this one, isn't it?" said Mary Ann. "Lots of steep stairs and landings and things. How's his wife doing?"

"She was right there when it happened, poor thing, or it would have been worse. She called the ambulance right away when she couldn't rouse him."

"How do you know so much about it?" asked Gertrude.

"I know his wife slightly. I met her at a party three or four years ago. She was a promising artist herself, but she seemed to just drop out of sight after she married him. She called me yesterday morning in a very agitated state and asked if I could help her. It seems that there have been strange things happening at the house. She's just about frantic with fear. For some reason she remembered my name and called me. She sounded pretty desperate. I guess the police have been questioning her quite closely as to the circumstances surrounding the fall, and that, along with the strange events, has completely unnerved her."

"So what's all this got to do with you?" asked Don.

"She wants me to come out there in my ghost-hunting capacity and see if I can find anything. I told her I'd get back to her tomorrow."

"I suppose we could make a diagnostic visit," said Mary Ann. "I am invited too, aren't I?"

"Of course you're invited, you're always invited," said Jim.

"Sounds interesting," said Gertrude. "I can go, can't I, Don?"

"As long as I can go too," said Don. "I still get the willies every time I think of that disappearing baby in New England."

"Well, it's Willie's house, so you may have to get them

again." Mary Ann grinned.

"As long as nothing happens to Gertrude. After all, I just found her!"

"Nothing is going to happen to her. She's only going to go there to get a psychic feel for the place for us so we'll know where to start. Maybe Molly and Lucy can give us a hand from the other side too."

"Oh, goody!" said Mary Ann. "Let's see if they're handy right now and ask them." She immediately began her trance-inducing routine.

"Hey! Slow down!" said Jim. "We don't even know what we want them to do yet. Let's set up an appointment to see Mrs. Poste first and go over and have a look around before we go involving the other side. Besides, we don't even know where Molly and Lucy are, or if they'll be able to help us."

"They're here right now. I just caught a glimpse of them before you called me back so abruptly. They're sitting over there on the clock shelf where they usually do."

Don and Jim couldn't prevent themselves from turning to look at the clock shelf even though they knew they were not sensitive enough to see the two spirits.

Gertrude laughed at their response. "You guys! You'd

think you could see them too."

"If you'd all be quiet, I'd like to try to get tranced again," said Mary Ann. "Do you want to come with me, Trudy?"

"Sure," said Gertrude, "I haven't seen Molly since before she died, and I'd like to ask her about Mom too." She relaxed her mind and began her deep breathing routine to induce her trance. Suddenly Lucy appeared on the shelf, but who was that pretty young woman with the flowing black hair and bright black eyes beside her? She was smiling at Gertrude and Mary Ann as if she knew them.

"Hello, Lucy, it's nice to see you again." Gertrude greeted the spirit on the right side of the shelf. "Who's your friend?"

"Humph!" said Molly. "Gertie doesn't even recognize her old nemesis. That's pretty bad."

"Molly!" cried Gertrude. "It's really you! My goodness, you've certainly changed."

"Of course I've changed. Did you think I'd stay looking like an old witch forever?"

"Well, yes, er, no, I don't really know what I thought," said Gertrude. "And please don't call me Gertie."

"Humph!" said Molly again, "that's probably the truth of the matter right there, you didn't think at all."

"Oh, I'm so excited!" chirped Mary Ann, as her consciousness arrived on the other side. "Did you two hear? We're all going on a ghost hunt. That is, if you want to."

"I guess we could give you a hand." Molly tried hard to keep the sparkle of anticipation out of her eyes.

"Give them a hand indeed," said Lucy. "You've never even been on a ghost hunt. You don't know the first thing about it!"

"I can imagine, can't I?"

"Imagine all you want, but don't make up stories for truth about it."

"Will you two quit your arguing please," said Gertrude. "I want to ask you a few questions before we have to go back."

"What d'you want to know?" asked Molly.

"Have you seen my mother?"

"No," said Lucy, "she's still asleep."

"Asleep?"

"Yes, she has a lot of healing to do before she's ready to take up her duties as a spirit. She was very confused when she came over. It was the result of her confusion in the physical."

"Then why is Molly up and about so soon?"

"Except for her broken hip and general weakness from the pain, she was essentially healthy. Her mind was alert so she didn't have to sleep as long. It takes much longer to heal when the mind is affected."

"Will I be able to see Mom when she does wake up?"

"I don't know. It depends on what her assignment is, and whether she wants to see you, and why you want to see her. She was only your mother in the physical, you know. Now she's a spirit like us, with work of her own to do. She may not think it's necessary to see you again."

"Oh," said Gertrude. "I find it difficult to understand that my mother wouldn't want to see me, and that she's not really my mother anymore."

"I'm sorry," said Lucy, "but that's the way it is. You'll understand better some day, and then it won't seem so hard."

"What's this about a ghost hunt?" said Molly.

"This guy had an accident," said Mary Ann, "and he's been in a coma, and the last couple of days strange things have been happening in his house. His wife is in the house alone and she's scared out of her wits."

"Who is he?" asked Molly.

"He's an artist, well-respected in the art circles."

"Why doesn't his wife just move out until he gets better? I don't have any patience for people who don't do the obvious," said Molly.

"She can't. She has nowhere to go. Her family has sort of abandoned her."

"Nasty old so-and-so's, weren't they."

"Molly! Watch your language. We don't use those kinds of expressions here."

"Why not? That wasn't a bad word. I could have used a lot worse."

"I know you could have, but those are earth standards and we have higher standards to attain to here. Besides, language like that takes away from your soul-stuff, and doesn't serve any useful purpose."

Gertrude chuckled to herself. So Molly has a thing or two to learn too, she thought. Aloud she said, "Back to this artist and his wife. She's very frightened in the house by herself, especially at night, and she's called Jim to ask him if he could get to the bottom of this apparent haunting. Do you want to help us?"

"Well, my dear," said Lucy, "if we can, we'll help you, of

course, only if it's a case of true haunting. If the party isn't dead it's not, and we really can't do anything from this side."

"Can't we go along anyway?" asked Molly.

"Now Molly, you know that would be meddling," said Lucy.

"Meddling! Why's everything that's fun meddling?"

"Molly, you know the rule about interfering in the lives of mortals."

"We interfered in Gertie's life plenty," said Molly. "I don't see what the difference is."

"Gertrude is one of us. A sensitive, and a very good one at that. Now, no more argument."

Molly subsided into a black silence.

Gertrude could feel her trance slipping away. "I have to go now," she said. "We'll investigate and see you later." She became aware of her physical surroundings again. She sat up straight and stretched. "Well, that was interesting," she whispered to Jim and Don, careful not to disturb Mary Ann who was still in trance.

After a few minutes Mary Ann sat up too, and looked around. "Lucy's sure got her hands full with that Molly. She was still pestering to come with us when I left. How much do you want to bet she'll show up, with or without Lucy?"

"I guess there's not much we can do about that," said Gertrude.

Mary Ann shrugged. "We can always ignore her, I suppose. Just pretend she's not there."

"That'd be kind of rude, wouldn't it?"

"Not if we didn't go into trance." Mary Ann got up and stretched her sturdy frame. "How about some coffee, Jim? I'm chilled to the bone. This traipsing back and forth to the spirit world is like sitting on an iceberg sometimes."

"We should go soon," said Don. "It's getting quite late." He rose to get their sweaters.

"Let us know what you decide to do," said Gertrude. "I don't want to miss this for anything."

Jim walked them to the door. "I'll call Mrs. Poste tomorrow and set up an appointment. If I know her state of mind, she'll want us over there tomorrow evening. Will you be able to make it on such short notice?"

Gertrude's eyes were sparkling. "Of course we can, can't we, Don."

Don laughed. "I suppose I have to agree."

CHAPTER TWO

The next day Don arrived home from work a little earlier than usual. The late afternoon sun through the stained glass in the front door warmed the austerity of the entrance and hallway of the old house. Gertrude met him at the door with her customary exuberance. "Mm," said Don, "that's how I like to be greeted. If I go outside and come in again can we do it over?"

Gertrude snuggled closer, her coppery curls, turned more coppery still in the light through the door, tickled the underside of his chin. "I have a better idea."

"I don't think we have time right now, not if we're going to go ghost hunting with Jim this evening."

Gertrude pulled back from his embrace. "Jim called?

What'd he say? What time are we going? Where are we going?"

Don laughed at her sudden change of direction. "Whoa, slow down. He wants us out at his place as soon after supper as we can get there. He wants to brief us first."

"Then I'd better get moving," said Gertrude. She turned and hastened toward the kitchen. "We don't want to be late for our very first ghost hunt."

I hope this is not all a big mistake, thought Don, as he went upstairs to change. All his old fears were returning, now that Gertrude's psychic abilities were actually going to be put to use. If anything happens to her, I don't know what I'll do, he thought as he remembered the apporting of the baby on his one and only ghost hunt in his college days.

The early summer sun was hanging low in the sky behind them as they made their way out to Jim's that evening. Its rays painted a red and gold path across the Northumberland Strait enhancing the redness of the soil. The whole landscape seemed to glow as they made their way to the top of Tea Hill. Passing the crest of the hill, the scene changed to misty grey as the hill behind them blocked the sun's brightness.

"I'm glad you took the old road instead of the

Trans-Canada," said Gertrude. "It's so beautiful to come over the top of the hill and see the ocean so misty and still after the brightness behind us."

"This is one of my favourite drives," said Don. "It gives me such a feeling of peace to come over the hill and see the farms and the marsh and then the ocean spread out beyond them."

They arrived at Jim's by seven o'clock. Mary Ann pulled in behind them, on time for once in her haphazard life. "This is going to be such fun. I'm so glad we discovered you and your talents," she babbled.

"Who discovered her?" said Don.

"Well," she amended, "you really discovered Gertrude, but we uncovered her abilities."

"Actually, I discovered him." Gertrude took Don's hand as they crossed the yard.

"Okay, okay." Mary Ann laughed. "We're here now and I'm looking forward to this expedition." She knocked on the door. Betsy woofed from somewhere inside. Presently Jim opened the door and Betsy rushed out, dancing in excited circles around their feet.

"She knows we're going on a ghost hunt," said Jim, as he let them in. "I don't know how she does it, but she always knows. It's the only thing she gets this excited about. I'm glad you got here this early, I have quite a few things I want to tell you before we start. Mrs. Poste is expecting us about seven-thirty, so we only have about ten or fifteen minutes to discuss the plan."

Gertrude could feel her skin begin to tingle. A real ghost hunt, she thought, I wonder what's going to happen.

Jim observed Don's worried face. "Now first of all, I want you to understand that ghosts can't hurt us because they're not of our plane. Their energy is only the remnants of the psychic energy their bodies contained when they were alive. They sometimes have enough strength to throw things and knock things over, but they can't directly harm us. Mind you, if they start throwing things, it would be prudent to duck!"

Don laughed nervously. How do I get myself into things like this anyway? He looked across at Gertrude's eager face. I never thought I'd be married to a psychic.

Jim continued, "I'm going to interview Mrs. Poste first.

Then I'll ask her to show us the house, especially the areas that seem to be affected. You guys can ask anything you want to know too. She seems very open and more than eager to have this thing solved."

"What do you want us to do?" Gertrude sipped her steaming coffee.

"Listen carefully to everything she says. Use all your senses to try to determine if she's telling the truth on all points. When we go on the tour of the house be open to any psychically hot spots. Mary Ann can show you how to do it. I'm going to be alert to any physical oddities about the place, in case this is all an elaborate prank made up just to scare her, or to lead us down the garden path. I'll spend a lot of time knocking on walls and panelling. According to her, it's a very old house so it probably has quite a bit of space unaccounted for in the walls. There may be a way for a prankster to get in and out without her knowing about it."

"A secret passage?" Gertrude opened her eyes wide. "Really?"

"Perhaps." Jim smiled. "If there are any, you're not to go exploring on your own. They can be very dangerous in those old houses, they may have rotted out or never been finished. They likely wouldn't have lights either, so Don and I will do any exploring of that nature."

"Only if you go first!" said Don. "I'm a complete coward when it comes to ghosts and darkness and hidden things. That apport was enough to last me a lifetime!"

Jim laughed. "I'll go first. Now we'd better get a move on if we expect to get there at the appointed time. Mary Ann, you'd better go with Don and Gertrude. I have my car packed with equipment and Betsy will be riding with me. You can show them how to get there." He went to the door and whistled for Betsy. She came bounding up and woofed. "Time to go, Betsy," said Jim. She pranced over to the mini, and pawed at the door handle.

"She's eager," said Don.

Jim closed the door behind the dog. "She knows where we're going, and she loves a car ride." He closed and locked the house. "See you there," he called, then climbed in beside Betsy.

Gertrude laughed. "That's the funniest thing I've seen in a long time, big Jim and Betsy in that little, tiny car. I never realized how much dog and master resemble each other."

Don started the motor. "It's sort of cartoon-like isn't it."

He backed around and followed Jim out the lane. "There's a whole pop psychology about how people choose pets that resemble them."

"In Jim's case, it really fits," said Mary Ann.

They arrived at the Poste household to find all the lights blazing, and Mrs. Poste standing in the middle of the lawn with a croquet mallet in her hands. She was in tears. "It's started again," she sobbed when they had assembled around her. "I turned all the lights on upstairs when it started to get dark. I thought it might discourage whoever or whatever was creating such havoc, but it hasn't done a thing."

"Why are the downstairs lights on?" asked Jim.

Mrs. Poste sniffed hugely and rubbed her nose with the heel of her hand. Mary Ann handed her a tissue. "I thought I heard the noise starting in the library, so I reached around the corner of the doorway and flicked on the light. I heard glass breaking in there so I ran out through the hallway and turned on those lights as I went. The kitchen lights and the living room lights were on already." She sniffed again.

"How long ago was this?" asked Mary Ann.

"About half an hour ago, I think," she replied. "It seems an awfully long time though." Her slight body was trembling.

"Has the noise stopped?" asked Jim.

"A few minutes ago it kind of quieted down in there. I'm so scared." She covered her face with her hands and burst into a fresh bout of sobbing, her long blond braid quivering with the energy of her weeping. "It's b-b-bad enough that he had to go and fall downstairs and knock himself unconscious, b-b-but the police think I pushed him, and now this." She sniffed again and tried to find a dry spot on her tissue.

Gertrude found a spare tissue in her pocket and handed it to her.

"Now, Mrs. Poste, if you can calm yourself a little, we need to ask you some questions," said Jim. The bumping and banging started again inside the house. Even out there on the lawn she had to raise her voice to answer him.

"I'm sorry I can't ask you in," she sniffled, "but you can hear for yourself what it's been like, although this is the worst yet." Another crash echoed from the house. She blew her nose loudly, and sniffed again. "I guess we could sit on the patio at the table there." She turned and led the way around the outside of the house.

It was an old building, unpainted, and weathered for the most part to a beautiful grey. It was of solid construction with peaks and steep roofs defining its upper profile against the evening sky. It had been renovated and added onto at various times during its existence, the latest addition being the patio with its sliding glass doors in back and the curved greenhouse windows on the sides. It stood at odds to the rest of the weathered structure. In the patio, baskets of plants hung from the ceiling, and the glass walls were lined with a variety of tropical trees and bushes. The fragrance of foreign blossoms thickened the air. The glass doors were partly open, for the day had been pleasantly warm. Mrs. Poste led the way inside.

"I've spent the day here," she said, "and it looks like I'm going to spend the night here too. It seems to be the only place that's not affected by this … whatever it is. I guess I'm lucky there's a couch here and that the nights are fairly warm now. I'm sorry I can't offer you anything, I don't dare go into the kitchen, but please sit down." She sniffed again.

The faux caned chairs scraped across the flagstones as

everyone found a seat. An old fashioned doily with a pot of English lavender decorated the centre of the round table. The disturbance from the house seemed to have settled down to an occasional thump and crash. Jim opened the interview.

"When did this all start?"

"Last week. I didn't realize what was happening at first. It all started with an occasional creak or thump. The heat would still come on at night sometimes, so I thought it was just the old furnace, or the house settling, or something." She sniffed again.

"When did you realize that it was more than that?"

She pulled her long braid around to the front and began playing with the tuft at the end. "A few days ago when I went upstairs to the studio I found a number of things disturbed, tubes of paint opened and lying on the floor, the easel upset, and the canvas that he was working on lying beside it on the floor, paint brushes scattered everywhere and all dried to a board. He was always very tidy about his studio, everything had a place and everything was in its place if he wasn't using it."

"You said this is the worst it's been?" prompted Jim. "When did the noise and disturbance come downstairs?"

"It got steadily worse in the attic, and yesterday the noise started in the dining room. It's been in the living room too and in the kitchen, but not all at the same time."

"Has there been a lot of damage done?"

"Not compared to the noise. Just because there's a sound of glass breaking doesn't mean that you'll find glass broken when you go to look. Sometimes there is though." She jumped to her feet and began pacing. Tears began dribbling down her cheeks again. She mopped at them with the now soggy tissue. "I'm a nervous wreck."

"Has anything valuable been destroyed?"

"No, anything that's been broken has been pretty insignificant." She collapsed into her chair again.

"It seems fairly quiet in there now. How about showing us around?"

A crash resounded throughout the house. Everyone jumped. Betsy howled, a mournful, chilling howl, her head thrown back to expose the white patch under her chin. Mrs. Poste paled more than ever. "I'm afraid to go in there," she whispered. "As soon as I think that I might be able to go back in, the noise starts up again."

"So it seems to be aware of what your intentions are?"

Mrs. Poste laughed wryly. "You should have heard it right after I called you the other day."

"I guess you don't mind if we take a look on our own?" asked Jim.

"No, of course not. The light switches are all beside the doors, I'd appreciate it if you would turn them off as you go. Maybe you would think to bring me a blanket from one of the beds too, then I won't have to go in there at all this evening." A weak smile warmed her thin features as she seemed to relax a little at the thought of not having to enter the house again that night.

"I'll go first," said Jim. "I don't want any of you to get hurt if there is something there that's not paranormal that might be dangerous." He started into the house. "C'mon Betsy. You can come too."

Betsy woofed once and trotted to her master's side, her great plumed tail waving. Together they entered the house by way of the patio, with the others close behind them.

They toured each downstairs room one by one. Every room was painted the same dull grey with white crown moulding. Some walls were papered in out-of-date flowers and scrolls, the colours not quite in harmony with the grey paint. The drapery on the windows was faded, and over everything was a thin layer of dust as if Mrs. Poste had not had the energy to keep up with such a large house. Betsy sniffed into every crack and corner she could find. Once she scratched and woofed at a space between the wall and a fireplace but there was nothing there.

In the library Mary Ann spent some moments looking at the array of old books on the shelves. "This is a very unhappy household," she said. "I get a sense of some very nasty arguments taking place in this room."

"They seem to be old arguments, though," said Gertrude. "I sense the disturbances in the ether too." She gazed around at the general dinginess of the room and took note of the dust beginning to hang from the two small chandeliers. "I wonder if they are connected to these people, or to previous owners?"

"I can't tell that just now. They seem to be coming from a long way back, so unless they've lived here for quite some time, it probably isn't them. Why don't you ask her how long she's lived here, Jim?"

"I plan to ask her all kinds of personal questions before I'm through here. I expect we'll even get to know why she's feeling so guilty about her husband's fall."

"You noticed that too, did you?" said Don. "There are several points that she's not being entirely candid about, I think."

Jim looked into every corner of the library, behind drapes and furniture, and under tables. He found nothing except more dust. The others followed closely behind. "What's this?" He stopped abruptly. "There're several books on the floor here." They all came to a halt in unison almost bumping into him in the process. "They look as if they've just been piled there. They're too neat." He took note of the titles. Turning around then, he nearly bumped into his shadows. "Will you guys quit it? There's nothing to be afraid of from the spirit world, and there's certainly nothing in here!"

"I know that," said Mary Ann.

"Then why are you following me?"

Mary Ann blushed. "I guess nervousness is catching."

Jim knocked on the walls around the built-in bookcases, and around the fireplace. "There doesn't seem to be any hollowness around here where you'd expect to find it." From where he was standing he could see under the edge of the lumpy, faded sofa. "Hm," he said, "this must have been what broke when she turned on the lights." He picked up a larger piece of glass and several smaller bits. "I guess I'd better save these, she may be able to identify them." He placed them carefully in his handkerchief.

Betsy sat waiting by the door, her tour of the room completed. "Okay, Betsy," said Jim. "let's look at something else." The dog trotted ahead of them and went into the living room. A thorough tour of this room revealed everything to be in reasonable order. Here the furniture seemed newer but was certainly not modern. The atmosphere seemed a little brighter here than in the library, but the same patina of dust covered everything. A magazine lay open on the footstool.

The second floor held four bedrooms, only one of which seemed to be in use. In that one the bed was unmade, the drapes hung awry, dresser drawers spilled their contents onto the floor, an uncapped perfume bottle lay on its side with the perfume half evaporated, clothing was strewn everywhere, and dust covered the lot.

"Wow," said Gertrude, "the housekeeping is a little lacking." She went into the adjoining bathroom. Here everything was pin neat and scrubbed. She came out looking puzzled.

"What'd you find?" asked Don.

"The bathroom. It's tidy. Go look at it."

The others trouped in to look at the bathroom. "You're right," said Jim, "it looks as if it has just been housecleaned."

"It will be nearly impossible to tell if anything is out of place here." Mary Ann looked around and compared it to the shambles in the bedroom. "Let's look in the attic."

"Just a minute, I still have to test the walls here." Jim began tapping his way around the perimeter of the room. A loud thump resounded in response to his tapping. Everyone jumped, including him. Betsy whined. The sound seemed to come from the head of the bed.

"Well," said Jim, recovering his calm, "that certainly brought a response." He tapped along the head of the bed. "There doesn't seem to be any hollowness here. I wonder what's behind this room?"

"It should be an outside wall, shouldn't it?" Don thought of the layout of the house. He leaned out the window. "We're right over the greenhouse," he called.

"I wonder if Mrs. Poste has anything to do with this?" said Jim.

"I don't think so," said Mary Ann, "I don't get a sense of her interference at all. What do you think, Gertrude?"

"I have no sense of anything happening connected with her. I sense her presence very strongly here in the bedroom, but nowhere else much, and especially not connected with that thumping," said Gertrude.

Don slammed the window shut. "As a mere mortal of very little talent, I think she's also a very frightened mortal of little talent in the spiritual sense. She was still sitting at the table playing with her braid."

"I think I'm reserving judgement until we find out what she's lying about," said Jim. "C'mon, let's check out the attic."

They all trouped up the hall with Betsy in the lead. Reaching the bottom of the stairs Betsy stopped abruptly, staring up the stairs at the closed door at the top of the landing. Her hackles rose, and a deep growl emanated from the depths of her furry throat. She tried to block the stairs.

"Well, I wonder what's there?" A note of curiosity crept into Jim's voice. "She doesn't very often react that way. Most of the time she's just happy to explore."

Betsy began sniffing excitedly around the newel post. "I

wonder if this is where he landed?" Jim started to climb the stairs. Betsy grabbed his pant leg in her teeth and growled.

"Huh!" said Don, "she certainly doesn't want you to go up there!"

"Betsy, let go!" commanded Jim. Betsy continued to hold onto his pant leg. Jim backed down the stairs and Betsy gave up her hold on his trousers. "Can you girls get a sense of anything up there?"

Gertrude and Mary Ann relaxed their minds and allowed impressions to come in. "Phew!" muttered Mary Ann, after a few moments, "that was some fight!"

"Recent too, I'd say," said Gertrude. She was almost in trance. "I don't see anything though."

"It must have been very brief, it doesn't seem to have left much visual impression behind."

"No," said Gertrude, "but the fight must have been pretty fierce, the air is still vibrating from the power of it."

They went up the stairs. Don went with them. "Wait! Let me go first." He pushed his way ahead of them. Betsy sat at the bottom with Jim's big hand firmly holding her collar. She whined, and strained to be free. "Stay!" commanded Jim. Betsy barked once, a sound sharp with fear.

Mary Ann opened the door and looked inside. The lights were still burning brightly, and little seemed displaced in the big sky-lighted room. Betsy broke free of Jim's hold on her collar and bounded up the stairs barking, with Jim following close behind. A loud barrage of knocking erupted from inside the room. A can of paint brushes soaking in turpentine fell over and spilled across the polished plank work table.

"I think we've found our 'hot spot,'" said Mary Ann. She found a rag and began mopping up the mess.

Jim joined them in their survey of the room. "Nice studio." A rap from the opposite wall seemed to agree with him. Betsy sat in the doorway and growled, refusing to do her usual tour of new surroundings. "Let's get started," said Jim. "I'll do a physical survey, and when I get done, you two can survey the ether."

"Impressions are coming thick and fast right now," mumbled Mary Ann, on the very edge of a trance. "There's a great deal of blackness in this room. Such unhappiness! Can't you feel it, Trudy?" A tear rolled down her cheek.

Gertrude breathed deeply. "It feels as if a heavy weight is pressing on my chest," she muttered in reply.

They roamed the room for some minutes but found nothing beyond the overwhelming sense of sadness of a life out of step with the spiritual, overlaid with fear. They returned from their investigation, tired and spiritually dishevelled.

"I've got to go downstairs." Gertrude returned her attention to the physical. "I can't stand this atmosphere anymore." She headed out the door.

"I'm with you." Mary Ann followed her.

Don made a move to go after Gertrude then stopped at the doorway and looked back. "Hurry up, will you."

Jim began his methodical survey of the room. Betsy sat in the doorway and whined. It was a light room despite the lateness of the hour and must have been full of sunlight during the day. Just now it was lighted by the brightness of fluorescent bulbs. A few daubs of paint dotted the work table and the floor around where the easel had stood. For an artist's studio it was very clean despite the mess created by the otherworldly energy. Nothing seemed damaged except for a few dried paint brushes that had lain out of their overturned soaking cans too long. Even the damp canvas that had fallen when the easel had been overturned had landed face up. Other paintings were neatly stacked against the walls. Others were in racks awaiting transport to Willie's next show.

Mary Ann and Gertrude waited in the hall for Jim and Don to return.

"I didn't see anything, did you?" asked Gertrude.

"No," said Mary Ann, "but the unhappiness in that room weighs a ton. I wonder what Wee Willie was like."

"Hard to say. I've only heard rumours, and not very many of those. None of them were very nice." Gertrude sat down on the bottom step and looked up at Mary Ann. "Some say he's very cruel, wicked even."

"I suppose we could always ask Mrs. Willie to describe him." Mary Ann laughed.

"You'd better be careful, calling her Mrs. Willie, you'll be calling her that to her face the next thing you know, and she may not like it." Gertrude chuckled then too, infected with a sense of relief at Mary Ann's return of lightheartedness.

Presently the two men came down from the studio.

"What'd you find?" asked Mary Ann.

"Not a thing. The place appears to have been built fairly recently, and nothing seems to be amiss in the construction.

I've measured everything just to make sure. I wonder if Mrs. Poste has a set of blueprints for the house somewhere?"

Betsy made a run for downstairs, her tail straight out behind her.

They all laughed at the sight. "She's sure anxious to get out of here," said Jim. "I've never seen her this eager before."

They rejoined Mrs. Poste on the patio. The house behind them was quiet for the moment.

"I've brought you a couple of blankets and a pillow," said Gertrude. "I thought it might get cold out here before morning, and I know I'm not comfortable without my pillow." She smiled at Mrs. Poste.

Mrs. Poste smiled wanly in return. "Thanks," she said, "it does still get cold at night, and please call me Connie." The last came out in a rush. "Hardly anyone calls me Connie anymore." She sighed.

"Well, Connie," said Jim, "this tour has brought a few questions to mind. First of all, do you know what this is?" He unfolded his hanky, exposing the bits of glass to the lamp light.

"I think it was Willie's glass ashtray that he got in Paris. It was sitting on the shelf in the library. It was special because he said that it drew the smoke in and kept the air clean. I never believed that. He's had it for years. Since before I came here."

"How long have you lived here?"

"Willie's lived here much longer than I have. He lived here with his first wife, but she left him. Then I came along. He hired me as a model for a big painting he was doing. I was modelling to pay my way through art school. The painting was a big success and he married me. That was eight years ago now." She looked back over the past. Her shoulders drooped.

"Why'd you marry him?" asked Don.

"He was kind to me, and I had no one. My parents kicked me out when I was eighteen. I was kind of a hellion in school, the only thing I wanted to do was to draw and paint, so as soon as I graduated they told me I had to find a place of my own. For all the running around I did, I still managed to get pretty good marks, so I applied to art school and began working as a model. That's how I came to be working for Willie."

"Do you know anything about these books in the library?" Jim recited the titles.

"No, those are Willie's, and I wasn't allowed to touch them except to dust them. Why?"

"They were stacked neatly on the floor behind the sofa."

Connie paled. "I know it doesn't look like it, but I dusted in there this morning and they were on the shelf. It was before all the noise started for the day."

"Could anyone have come into the house without you knowing about it?"

"I don't think so. The doors were all locked except for this one and I was in the greenhouse most of the day. I would have seen anyone coming in, or at least have heard them."

"What was Mr. Poste like?"

Connie shrugged. "He was a very able artist. His professional reputation was international."

"You mentioned earlier that the police seem to think that you pushed him."

"Well, I didn't," said Connie. "We'd had a disagreement and he missed his footing and fell." A bleak look crossed her face as she recalled the exact sequence of events. Don observed the display of thoughts as they crossed her face in quick succession.

"I'm sorry to upset you, Connie," said Jim, "but I need

to know as much as you're willing to tell me about Mr. Poste if I'm to sort out the origin of the noises and breakage. Do you know anything about the previous owners? This is a very old house, so there must be a number of them."

"I only know about Willie and his first wife."

"Do you have a copy of the deed?"

"No, Willie kept all that in a safety deposit box at some bank in town."

Jim frowned. "Didn't you have access to important papers and bank accounts?"

Connie seemed to shrink into her chair. "No, he always told me that it was none of my business, that he'd take care of it."

Gertrude could keep silent no longer. "But what about your personal needs? He did provide for those, didn't he?"

Connie looked at her from under her lashes. "He made me an allowance."

"Was your marriage a happy one?" asked Don. "You're quite a bit younger than he is, I see."

"I'm twenty-seven. He's fifty-seven." She didn't elaborate further.

"But were you happy together?" persisted Don.

Connie glared at him. "What's happy like? He looked after me. I wasn't starving, and I wasn't cold. I had a place to come into out of the rain."

"Happy is a lot more than that." Don looked across the table at Gertrude.

Just then the telephone rang. Connie got up to answer it. Her face paled alarmingly. All Gertrude's nursing instincts rushed out as she ran to Connie's side. "Whatever is wrong?" she asked.

"It's Willie. He's taken a turn for the worse. I have to go." She hurried into the kitchen to get her purse. For once the house was silent.

CHAPTER THREE

After they left Connie's house, the four friends and colleagues reconvened in Jim's kitchen. Betsy flopped down with a huge doggie sigh in front of the stove that was still slightly warm from supper, her favourite place after a hard evening of ghost hunting. Mary Ann stirred the ashes from the suppertime fire and found a few embers still glowing. She stoked up the fire and added some more wood, and soon it began to pop and crackle as the twigs and branches from last year's windfall caught fire. Jim clattered around in the pantry getting coffee ready to perk. Presently he returned to the kitchen.

"So, what did you guys think?" he asked. They all began to talk at once. "Whoa, slow down, one at a time. You first, Mary Ann. I notice you didn't have much to say during the interview, but I sure could see the wheels turning."

"Smelled rubber, did you?" Mary Ann laughed. "I'm not surprised. I was trying to get a fix on her level of honesty but I was having difficulty."

"I know what you mean," said Don. "I notice she didn't directly answer your question about the character of Mr. Poste. I think she's hiding something there."

"She wasn't very forthcoming about the fall, either," said Gertrude. "If she was that way with the police, it's no wonder they think she pushed him."

"D'you think she pushed him?" Jim brought in the coffee and accompaniments.

"No." Gertrude reached for her mug. "I think she'd have liked to."

"What makes you say that?"

"Well, any man who puts his wife on an allowance, and doesn't permit her to take part in the family finances, especially to the extent of even keeping the bank account location secret, has got to be some kind of a tyrant. I'm beginning to think that all those stories we heard about them are true. It makes me curious about what she's living on just now. It's been about a month since he fell, she must be out of money soon."

"I agree with Gertrude," said Mary Ann. "I can't quite get a fix on her psychically. The impressions I keep getting are of chaos. I'd say she's pretty upset, and trying to hide it."

"But you don't know if that's what he really did, or if that's just her perception of the situation, or if it's all just pure gossip. You know how PEI is," said Don, "what one knows, all know. I wonder how they got along together?"

"What does she do out there in the country all day if he's painting?" Mary Ann took another bite of cookie.

"I'd guess she's very bored," said Gertrude. "There were no signs of any kind of handicrafts, or books to interest a woman, or magazines except for that one that was open on the footstool."

Jim was busy taking notes. "My big question is, why did he and Mrs. Poste number one divorce? Who is she? Where is she now?"

"Is there any way we can find out these things without having to ask Connie? I don't like delving into people's pasts without their permission," said Gertrude.

"I suppose we could ask at the art college," said Mary Ann. "I'm acquainted with the director there, and he might be able to tell me."

Jim looked surprised. "How d'you know him?"

"I met him at a party one evening a few years ago. I'd been hired to tell fortunes for the guests, and he had his cards read. That was during my poor era."

"D'you suppose he'll remember you?" asked Gertrude.

"Oh, I think he will. He could hardly forget. I told him his wife of fifteen years was going to have a baby girl the following year, when they'd given up all hope of ever having children."

"And did they?" asked Gertrude.

"They did, and another the year after too. Funny thing, though," said Mary Ann, "I didn't see the second one coming." She began reaching for her fifth cookie.

"Have another cookie, Mary Ann." Jim smiled and lifted an eyebrow at Mary Ann.

Mary Ann looked at the one that was half eaten in her hand. "No, thanks, I'm watching my waistline." She chuckled.

"Does anyone have anything else to add?" asked Jim. "I'm plumb out of questions myself."

"Yes," said Gertrude, "I have one very important one. Where were Molly and Lucy this evening? I thought for sure they'd be there no matter what."

"That's right," said Mary Ann, "we didn't even catch a glimpse of them!"

"Well, guys." Jim yawned and stretched. "I hate to throw you out in the cold so to speak, but tomorrow's another day, and I'm beat. I want to try to track down the previous owners tomorrow, so I'm going to need all my strength."

Molly and Lucy were, in fact, very busy that evening. After choir practice, Larry was called away to a meeting from which he returned looking very grave. He found Molly and Lucy sitting on the gate that separated the approach to heaven through the daisy field from the side from which there was no return. They were enjoying the last of the sunshine. By swinging their feet they were able to make the gate sway like a swing.

"Why's this gate here?" asked Molly.

"D'you remember coming through here?" asked Lucy.

Molly looked around. "Can't say's I do. When was that?"

"We came in through these gates the day you came over,

but you were getting pretty sleepy by that time. Hardly anyone remembers coming here."

"Can we go down there?"

"If you want to. The field slopes down into a valley with a little river running through it."

"Is that where we came across? I seem to remember a bridge."

"Yes, that's where you make the decision to go back or stay. I work on the other side of the bridge helping people make the correct decision for themselves. Sometimes we tell them to go back, that they have more work to do in the physical, sometimes we tell them to come in. On very specific occasions we allow people who meet certain criteria to live in the daisy field while we work on them. Then when our work is complete, we send them back to live out the remainder of their lives in their newly adjusted state. It's made all the difference for some people to have spent time in the daisy field."

"What's Larry got to do with all this?"

"He oversees immigration workers. As a special subsection of his job description he gets to supervise the work of psychics and sensitives in the physical. I think he actually likes that part of his work better. It really is more interesting."

"What do you have to do with Larry?"

Lucy sighed. "I was assigned to keep him out of social trouble. He's very abrupt by times, especially when he really shouldn't be. It's been a full time job, I can tell you."

"So what do you do exactly?"

"Apologize mostly. I seem to always be smoothing someone's ruffled feathers, so to speak."

"Speaking of Larry, I think he's looking for us." Molly looked behind herself. "There he is, and in a hurry too."

"Over here, Larry," they shouted. He wafted over and joined them on the gate. "You're looking serious," they said almost in unison. "The meeting was kind of heavy-duty, was it?"

"It wasn't a meeting as such," said Larry. "It was just me and three of the elders. There's a guy coming across this evening who's not going to be staying very long. He's a mess, I guess, from what the elders said. They assigned him to us. D'you think you two are up to it?"

"Hot dog!" cried Molly, "My first case." She nearly lost her seat on the gate in her excitement.

Lucy smiled and asked, "What do we have to do for him?"

"Look after him," began Larry, as a loud moo and some thrashing noises erupted from the bottom of the hill. The valley was in dark shadow by that time of the evening, and nothing could be seen.

"We don't have cows down there, do we?" asked Lucy.

"We don't have cows, period." Larry wafted off the gate. "C'mon, let's go see what's up."

The three spirits floated toward the racket and discovered a human spirit with its frayed silver cord tangled in the bushes. It moaned again, a long calf-like moo.

Molly and Lucy looked at each other. "D'you suppose it's in pain?" asked Lucy.

"Ugly, isn't it!" said Molly. She looked at the porcine body with the pock-marked face and bulbous nose.

"Help me get him straightened out, will you," said Larry. "He's fighting me."

Together the three spirits managed to extricate the newcomer from the mess he had arrived in without breaking the weakened cord. All the while he moaned more loudly and horribly. At last they were able to carry him up the hill and sit him on the grass, where he curled into a ball and rocked himself back and forth.

"I think this is our new assignment," said Larry.

"Oh, dear!" said Lucy.

"Oh, boy!" said Molly.

"Who is he?" asked Lucy.

"He's an artist from the other side. He fell downstairs a few weeks ago and hit his head. He's been in a coma ever since. This evening he took a turn for the worse. It'll be several weeks before we can send him back." Larry picked up the frayed cord and examined it. "You could say he was just hanging on by a thread. He's probably the one that Gertrude and Mary Ann were talking about the other evening."

Molly laughed.

Lucy asked, "What are we supposed to do with him in the meantime?"

Larry was silent for a moment. His big hands continued to run the damaged cord through his fingers as if he could heal it. He sighed. "He has some lessons to learn here before he goes back."

"How're we supposed to teach him anything in that condition?" asked Molly. "All he does is lay there and moo.

He sounds like a cow in heat!"

"Nevertheless," said Larry, "that's our assignment. I'm sure you girls will think of something." He wafted away over the fence. "I'll be back in a few minutes," he called.

"Humph!" said Molly, "you'd better be! In the meantime what are we going to do with mooly here?"

"Just watch him. I guess," said Lucy. "He seems pretty quiet now. I wonder what his mortal name is?"

"He has a hospital bracelet on." Molly managed to turn the bracelet to the light without disturbing their patient. "It says his name is William Poste. Wasn't that Gertrude and Mary Ann's case?"

Lucy nodded. "It was and I wonder if the haunting was what caused his fall."

Just then Willie rolled over onto his knees with a great groan and began scrambling away down the hillside on his hands and knees.

"Catch him!" Lucy took off after him as fast as she could float. Molly was close behind her, and together they seemed to be gaining on him until Lucy reached for him and tangled her energy field with his. Willie moaned more loudly, and lost his balance. He began to tumble over and over down the hill with Lucy wrapped up with him.

"Oh! Oh! Help me!" shouted Lucy, as they rolled faster and faster down the hill with Molly chasing them. Lucy and Willie finally fetched up against a spruce tree at the bottom of the field. "Ugh! Get him off me!" implored Lucy. "He's filthy!"

Molly disentangled their energy fields and helped Lucy to her feet. Willie lay on his back under the tree, and whimpered piteously.

"Whew!" said Lucy, "that was awful! He smells!" She brushed the spruce twigs and grass out of her hair and smoothed her skirt. "I suppose this skirt will never be the same again. I'll have to manifest another one. Darn! I liked this one especially well."

Willie moaned again.

"What are we going to do with him?" asked Mollie. "We can't just leave him here."

"No," said Lucy, "we're stuck with him until they decide he's ready to go back."

"We could make it unpleasant enough here so that he'll want to go back sooner," said Molly.

Lucy laughed. "It's tempting, but I don't think it would

go over very well with Larry and the elders. Besides, he has a lesson to learn while he's here."

Willie moaned again and rolled over onto his knees, snuffling around the base of the spruce tree like a pig looking for truffles.

"We'll have to keep a close eye on him, we can't trust him to stay put," said Lucy. "I wish Larry would get back, he might have some ideas."

"Put him on a leash?" said Molly.

"Who? Larry or Willie?" Lucy laughed.

"Both of them! Imagine that Larry deserting us when we most need him." Molly plunked herself down on the grass.

"I didn't desert you." Larry suddenly appeared beside Lucy. "I was checking out the shock treatment facilities. We weren't expecting anyone so soon who would need a treatment. I wanted to make sure there was someone there this evening."

"You might have said," replied Molly. "We had no idea when or if you were coming back."

"I said I'd be right back, didn't I?"

"Will you two cut out your bickering," said Lucy. "We need to do something about this unfortunate creature before he tries to get away on us again."

"What's this about shock treatments?"

Lucy and Larry both began to explain at once. "I'm the teacher," said Larry. "I'll do the explaining!"

Lucy subsided into silence. Larry began his explanation.

"Whenever anyone comes over in the condition that he's in, we can either let him sleep it off, or we can use electrotherapy to speed up the process. In his case he has to go back to the other side, so we're on a time schedule and the process needs to be speeded up."

"What's the matter with him?"

"He's led such a miserable life in terms of relationships, he's completely dirtied his soul stuff. Fortunately for him he's being given an opportunity to try to repair some of the damage. The people whom he's hurt the most are still alive so he has that option."

Lucy looked down at Willie who had curled himself into a ball at the base of the spruce tree and appeared to be sleeping. "Is that why he's so grey?" She reached out and touched him gently on the side with her foot. Willie moaned softly.

"That's why he's so grey," said Larry. "C'mon now, let's

try to get him over to the therapy room. Lucy, you take his head, Molly take his feet, and I'll take what I can of the middle. If he doesn't fight us we should be able to get him there without too much trouble."

"Where're we headed?" asked Molly.

"Up the hill and to the left of the gate." Larry pointed the way.

Molly looked at the two story white building that she had not noticed before. It seemed to merge with the wall as if it were part of it. The lights appeared in the first floor windows, then after a few moments the upper level lights came on.

"They're expecting us," said Larry. "We'll have to hurry."

They unrolled Willie from his foetal position. He moaned loudly and made a few feeble efforts to fight them off, but finally with a deep snoring sigh he subsided into a sleep-like state again. They hoisted his fat body and carried him up the hill in stages to the therapy room and laid him on the stretcher.

"Whew!" Larry took a moment to catch his breath when they had arranged him there. "He's heavy, even without his physical body."

"He must have done some really cruel things in his lifetime for his spirit to weigh so much." Lucy bent over and took in great gulps of air. "I must be in worse shape than I thought."

"We should have gotten the stretcher to begin with. I'm sweating as badly as he is." Molly's breath came in gasps as well.

They wheeled Willie to the elevator and rose to the second floor. In a moment they had transferred Willie to the treatment table.

The electrotherapy team had already arrived and had begun preparations for Willie's treatment. "You'll have to wait downstairs while we do this," said the head therapist putting on a light asbestos-lined suit. "We fill the whole room with energy and without special suits you wouldn't be able to stand it."

"Why? What happens during a treatment?" asked Molly. She looked at all the dials and lights on the control panel and pushed at one of the buttons. The machine began a low hum.

"Leave things alone," said the head technician. He pushed a few more buttons and the humming stopped.

"The treatment realigns energy and charges it up to where he can think coherently again and you can work with him. If you were in here without protection, because you're already in alignment, it would disrupt your energy field and you'd be rendered unconscious for some time. You might even need to be realigned yourself to be able to function normally again. So don't mess with the equipment."

Willie moaned. The therapist made a face as he strapped Willie to the table. "I guess the sooner we get on with this the better," he said. "He sounds in a bad way." He shooed the three spirits out of the room.

They made themselves comfortable in the barren waiting room of the oldest building in the area. It had seen heavy use over the centuries and had had only minimal upkeep. The walls were an unpleasant hospital grey. The door jambs were scuffed and dented from years of stretcher collisions with them. A potted palm sat in one corner needing much attention. A few dog-eared magazines were scattered on the coffee table. Lucy shuffled through them. They were all out of date.

In a few minutes a low hum began to build in the upper story. Willie moaned again, audible even at that distance.

The hum grew louder and the lights dimmed. Willie moaned more loudly still.

"I'm glad I'm not him," said Molly in the semi-darkness.

"It does sound painful." Lucy drew her knees up under her chin and hugged them tightly.

"It's not as bad as it sounds," said Larry from his seat in the corner behind the palm tree. "I had to have it done once."

"You did?" said Lucy and Molly in unison surprise.

Larry folded his arms across his broad chest, and smiled faintly. "Yes, I did."

"Well, tell us!" demanded Molly.

"I accidentally floated through an energy field and it disrupted my spiritual alignment. The spirit I was chasing got away. He was a bad one who'd come over and we were trying to get him to lie down and go to sleep for awhile and he was resisting. He finally broke free and escaped. I chased him and got caught in the field. It took them three earth days to find me and by that time I was in pretty hard shape. It took some serious work to rehabilitate me."

Molly looked worried. "These energy fields are dangerous then?"

"Not any more. There were a couple of other spirits

who got caught and they finally marked them so well, you couldn't miss them if you tried. You'll learn about them when you start classes tomorrow evening."

The humming from the therapy room lessened and finally stopped. The lights brightened, and a few moments later the door opened and the therapist brought in a dishevelled Willie. "Where am I?" He looked around the waiting room.

"You're on the other side." Lucy rose from her chair and went to take his arm.

"The other side of what?" He shrugged Lucy roughly away. She toppled into the potted palm.

Larry rose to his full height from behind the palm and stood towering over Willie in terrible wrath. "You will not behave that way toward anyone here," he boomed, "and especially not to my girls. You will apologize to Lucy at once, and help her out of the flower pot!"

Willie wilted. "Sorry," he said in a low voice.

"LOUDER!" roared Larry.

"I'M SORRY!" shouted Willie in terror. He floated over and offered a grimy paw to Lucy who had managed to struggle to a sitting position underneath the palm tree.

"Now. While you're with us on this side you will behave

like a gentleman with courtesy and kindness. You will do as I tell you without argument, and when you've proven that you're ready, we'll allow you to go back." Larry glared at Willie who gulped and blinked. "Do you understand me?"

"Y-yes," replied Willie.

"What's that? I didn't hear you!" Larry advanced on Willie who retreated several steps looking wildly about for some avenue of escape.

"Y-yes, sir?" Willie could not find a way out either verbally or physically.

"That's better," growled Larry. "We're going to take you to see a little show in a few minutes and you're to behave yourself and pay attention."

"But where am I?" Willie was almost in tears.

"Essentially, you're dead," said Molly from her perch of safety on the curtain rod.

"Dead! But I was just talking to Connie a few minutes ago."

"That was last month. You had a fall and have been in a coma ever since." Larry glared in Molly's direction. "You're not dead yet, but if you pass through those gates over there, you can never return to the physical as William Poste."

Willie sat down on the sofa. "But this seems so real! You seem so real!"

"Of course we're real," said Lucy. "We're just as real here as you are in the physical."

"Why am I here then?"

"You've been given another chance," said Larry. "It's lucky for you, we maintain a complete spiritual health care complex on this side of the gate for people like you."

"What's that?" asked Willie.

"It's like a hospital, a rehabilitation centre, if you will, where people with serious spiritual defects come to learn better ways of coping. It's where people who are on the brink of death can get a second shot at earth life to right some of the wrongs they've done. You're one of the lucky ones, not everyone gets to do this."

"Why me?"

Larry snorted. "It's certainly not because you merit it any more than some of these other poor slobs who come over, it's merely because the people you need to make reparations to are still in the physical."

"Oh," said Willie. "Was I that bad?"

"Worse," said Larry.

"Come with Molly and me," said Lucy, taking Willie's dirty grey sleeve. "We have a movie to show you."

CHAPTER FOUR

The telephone rang early at Jim's house the next day. It was Mary Ann.

"I just wanted to check with you before I go to see Max Perry at the art college. Is there anything you'd especially like to know?"

"Just what we talked about last evening," said Jim. "Why don't you take Gertrude with you, she'd probably enjoy meeting him and she may be able to pick up some vibes while you're talking to him."

"What a good idea. We can go to that new restaurant

on Queen Street for lunch afterwards. I hear the menu is scrumptious."

Jim laughed. "Still watching your waistline, are you, Mary Ann?"

"Somebody has to. Talk to you later."

An hour later Gertrude and Mary Ann climbed the wide granite staircase that led to the colonnaded main doorway of the Maritime College of Art.

"I've never been here before." Gertrude was a little awed by the imposing entry.

"Impressive, isn't it?" said Mary Ann, as they reached the top. "Stop for a moment and catch your breath. Now turn around and look."

The college was built beside the Hillsborough River, downstream from the bridge, and commanded a view of most of Charlottetown. Spread out below the broad steps, the park surrounding it stretched for what seemed like a half a mile. A small staff of gardeners kept the grounds and flower beds in showplace condition. Red sandstone walks threaded their way beneath the trees. At intervals along the paths, stone benches were placed for the weary or meditative. Beyond the garden glimpses of the river could be seen shining through the trees. In the distance the windows of the buildings of downtown twinkled in the sunlight. The small houses of the residential areas surrounded these like chicks around the mother hen. In the distance the tall spires of St. Dunstan's basilica were visible against the brightness of the sky. The air was crystal clear today as always.

Gertrude gasped. "I never thought our town was so beautiful."

"It is beautiful." Mary Ann turned and opened the door for Gertrude. "C'mon Trudy, I told Max we'd be here at nine-thirty."

They walked down the marble hall, their feet echoing on the floor.

"Where're the students?" asked Gertrude.

"This is the administration building, the classrooms and studios are all out back." She turned in at a doorway. "This is it here." She opened a frosted glass door. A minute later they were being welcomed into Max Perry's office.

"I never did get to thank you properly for that prediction you made about my child," said Max. "I'll never run down fortune tellers again."

"I'd be careful," said Mary Ann. "They're not all to be trusted and you can never tell which ones aren't honest."

"I guess you're right," agreed Max. "So what brings you ladies here today?"

"We're working with Jim MacDonald," she began.

"Jim the Ghost Hunter? Well, well, that must be very interesting." Max raised his right eyebrow. "So what can I do for you?"

"I'm getting to that," said Mary Ann. "This matter must be treated with the utmost discretion, you understand."

"To be sure, to be sure." Max's goatee quivered in the excitement of hearing some gossip. "I'm as safe as a bank."

Gertrude smiled a secret little smile to herself. Mary Ann continued, "We've been investigating some abnormal activity out at Willie Poste's and we need some background information about him. We can't ask his wife, she doesn't seem to know very much anyway, and what she does know she's not willing to tell."

The goatee was still. An expression of seriousness descended onto Max's cheery, gnome-like features. "I'm not surprised," he said. "I warned her though, and she didn't listen, so there wasn't much I could do but wish her well and hope for the best."

"What did you warn her about?"

"That the gossip about old Willie was pretty true, he's a mean old bugger. Treats women like dirt, and seems to truly enjoy it."

"How d'you know Connie?"

"She was a student here about eight years ago. She modelled for the freshman classes for extra money. She was a very promising artist. She was good enough to eventually make her living at it. I haven't seen her since she and Willie got married."

"What d'you know about Willie?"

"I roomed with him at art college. If you want to get psychological about it all, I think his attitudes stemmed from the way his mother treated them all when they were growing up."

Gertrude's ears perked up. She'd have to remember all this and ask Don about it when she got home.

Mary Ann laughed. "When in doubt, blame the mother."

"Well, in this case I think it was true."

"How so?"

"They were never allowed to relate in a normal fashion.

You know how kids do. Get into fights and scream and yell at each other for awhile and then it all blows over. She used to force them to talk softly all the time and they were never allowed to shout or wrestle. There was no way for them to get their anger out so it all stayed inside. My, how those kids hated their mother! She ruled them with an iron fist. They didn't dare talk back, or even mutter under their breaths. She had many ways of making them pay for disobedience, and none of it was physical. She didn't believe in spanking. Willie used to brag about how soft-spoken his family was and never realized the implications."

"Wow!" said Gertrude, "it's amazing what makes people tick."

"Where was his father during all this?" asked Mary Ann.

"Dad was there. A mere shadow of a man. He was completely under her thumb too. Willie vowed that he'd never let any woman treat him that way. He told me that himself one night after lights out."

"I wonder what his first wife was like," said Gertrude.

Max's goatee seemed to bristle. "She's a wonderful woman. He treated her just awful. I should know, I'm married to her!"

"Oh." Mary Ann was at a loss for words for a change.

"Yes, oh," said Max. "We were all good friends in college. I wanted to marry her then, but Willie spoke for her first so I couldn't say anything. She married him and they lived together out at that ramshackle place for ten years until he finally drove her away. She had no place to go. Her family never liked Willie and kind of turned their backs on her after they got married. Mind you, Willie didn't encourage them to come around anyway, in fact he finally turned them out. I had just started here as director so when she had no one to turn to, she thought of me. I was more than glad to oblige, and after one horrendous fight with Willie, he consigned both her and me to the hot place and we haven't spoken since. Not that that's any great loss as far as I can see."

"So tell me again how Connie got mixed up with him," said Mary Ann.

"She was a student here. She was existing on scholarships and what she could earn as an artist's model. She said one time at a low moment that her parents threw her out when she turned eighteen. I guess she kind of raised the devil in high school. Her grades were pretty good, not brilliant, except for the one in art. She could already paint up a storm and began getting scholarships for her work. I tried to make work here for her as much as I reasonably could, which is why she started modelling in the first place. Willie got wind of her through art circles. She was very beautiful when she was that age, kind of pure and innocent. Anyway, Willie was commissioned to paint that big mural at the new Federal building downtown, and he needed a model and he came after her."

"I thought I'd seen her somewhere before," said Gertrude.

"I tried to warn her about him. Discreetly, of course, but she either didn't get the message, or chose to ignore it. The next thing I knew, she'd dropped out of school and they'd gotten married. That was the last I heard of her."

"Do you think it would be useful to talk to your wife?" asked Gertrude.

Max shrugged. "She probably won't tell you much different than I've already told you. She doesn't like to talk about that period of her life, and I don't encourage her to. She was in therapy for several years after she divorced him, just to get her life back on track, and since then she's mostly put it behind her, as much as anyone can."

Mary Ann rose from her chair. "Well, thank you for all

your help. It's given us somewhere to start."

Max rose too. "What do you suppose is going on out there?"

"There's something happening that Connie can't handle and won't talk about. We're not even sure if she understands it all. She's very tight lipped."

Max chuckled, his goatee quivering in his amusement. "That's Connie alright. She never did talk much." He held the door open for them. "I hope you're successful with whatever it is out there. I sure hate to see Connie in such a mess, she's had a hard enough time already."

"It is too bad," said Mary Ann, "but you've been more than helpful, so perhaps we can unravel the mystery. Thanks again." They closed the outer door behind themselves and retraced their steps along the echoing marble halls.

"That was some story," said Gertrude.

"It sure was, though I've heard stranger." Mary Ann changed the subject abruptly. "Let's go have lunch at that new place on Queen Street. I hear their Shepherd's Pie is just heavenly."

The menu at Aunt Charlotte's Place proved to be every bit as good as predicted. The sunny room with its tables covered with red-checked oilcloth was reflected in the two large mirrors suspended from the old-fashioned picture rail. Real geraniums blooming redly on the window sills created an air of down home comfort.

"Mm," said Mary Ann digging into her Shepherd's Pie, "just the way I like it, crusty potatoes, real ones, not reconstituted, and the interior good and juicy and not too spicy." She took another bite.

"I'm just amazed that you're not as fat as a little pig, the way you eat sometimes."

"I only eat like this when there's something good to eat, like at Jim's. The rest of the time I'm very moderate in my meals, and I almost never eat junk food."

"Maybe I should adopt that practice. These baked beans are just delicious, and the brown bread tastes homemade. I wonder if the owners are Islanders?"

"Dunno," replied Mary Ann around a mouthful of Shepherd's Pie, "but I predict that this place will become popular in a very short time." She became quite serious for a moment. "I think it may even expand and change locations."

"How do you do that?" asked Gertrude in amazement. "You just seem to toss off these predictions with hardly a thought about them. Do they all come true?"

Mary Ann shrugged. "Some do, some don't. I think this one has a good chance of coming true."

"What makes you say that?"

"Well, look at what they've got here. Good cooking, plenty of it, a must in our hard-working society; a reasonable location, though the parking's not great. It'll be a great tourist attraction. There'll be busloads of them. Why wouldn't they succeed, especially once their reputation spreads?"

Gertrude laughed. "Oh, you! That wasn't a prediction at all. You just added up all the positives of the situation and made a 'prediction.' Anyone could do that."

"Exactly! The only difference between my predictions and the predictions of the general public is that I use a large helping of intuition, which gives me an edge in the prediction department."

"D'you mean that anyone could learn to do it?"

Mary Ann scraped up the last of her gravy with her spoon. "Yes, anyone can do it, they just think they can't. Of course, it's like anything else, some people have more of a talent for it than others."

"D'you suppose I could do it?"

"I don't see why not. You certainly have that kind of ability in other areas. Why don't you try?"

"What'll I try on?"

"Well, for instance, why not make a prediction about how you think this Poste case is going to turn out. We could write it down and compare the results when we've solved the case."

"Okay, just let me think for a minute."

"No, don't think actively. Just let the impressions come."

Gertrude was silent as she relaxed her mind. "All I'm getting is confusion," she complained after a few minutes.

"Try again and look beyond the confusion for the major elements of the situation."

Gertrude closed her eyes and tried again. "I see a man hanging from the rafters," she mumbled presently. "There's a baby and an old grandmother, they're rocking. Oh, no! She dropped it!" Gertrude's eyes flew open. "That was terrible. That old woman dropped that baby on its head deliberately."

"Calm yourself, there's nothing you can do now. Or then either for that matter." Mary Ann looked at Gertrude in wonder. "You know you've just done something that I'd give my eye teeth to be able to do."

"What's that?"

"You just psyched out a house from a distance. I've never been able to do that, not even in an emergency when I've had extra energy. I'm so glad I've found you."

Gertrude sat up straighter in her chair and changed the subject. "D'you suppose it's the souls of that poor little baby and the man in the attic that are haunting the place?"

"I wouldn't be surprised," said Mary Ann. "Probably the grandmother's still lingering too, if she really did drop him."

"Do you know how it's going to come out?" asked Gertrude.

"No, I don't usually bother for myself. Other people always want to know. The ones who believe they can't do it for themselves." Mary Ann paused to flag down the waitress. "I hear they have a wide selection of exotic coffees here. D'you want to try one?"

"Sure," replied Gertrude. "I think I'd like to try a French coffee, maybe espresso."

"It's pretty strong if you've never had it before."

"Maybe it'll bolster up my psychic juices." She laughed.

"So, what do you think of things so far? Not psychically speaking."

"I honestly don't know what to think." Gertrude stirred sugar into her coffee to try to mellow it a little.

"I don't know either. I get the sense that that house has a long history of unhappiness. The psychic imprint is there. Maybe Willie and Connie have triggered it, and since Willie isn't there right now, Connie gets to reap the results all by herself."

"You mean that if Willie were there he'd be subject to the same manifestations?"

"Yes, however, that's just one thought on the subject. Maybe it's all a set-up. Maybe there's nothing psychic about it at all."

"But who'd do a thing like that?"

Mary Ann shook her head. "If local gossip has it right, Willie's made enough enemies in this lifetime to do him for two or three lifetimes. Someone may be trying to get back at him, and Connie just got caught in the cross-fire."

Gertrude sipped her coffee. "You don't suppose that Connie's behind all this, do you?"

Mary Ann thought for a moment. "No, I honestly don't think she's behind any of it in a directive sort of way. If anything, the phenomenon is feeding off the energy generated by her unhappiness and their fights."

"Sort of like a poltergeist?"

"Mm, I guess you could call it that."

CHAPTER FIVE

Come in," called Jim from the kitchen that same afternoon.

"What are you, psychic or something?" Mary Ann let herself into the room. "I didn't even knock."

"Getting good, aren't I?" said Jim.

"You're fooling me," said Mary Ann. "… Aren't you?" She peered closely at Jim's smiling face. She pulled the rocker out of the direct sunlight so she could see him better and sat down.

Jim's eyes twinkled. He left her in suspense for a few moments, then he said, "I saw you coming across the fields, and Betsy woofed and went back to sleep, so I knew when you got here."

"Oh," said Mary Ann, "I was half afraid you were developing your miniscule psychic powers on me." She relaxed into the cushions on the rocker and began to rock.

Jim's face sobered. "Would that be so bad?"

Mary Ann thought it over for a few minutes. "No-o," she said at last, "not so bad in itself."

"What then?"

"Nothing." She ducked her head.

"Come on now, tell Uncle Jim. He can fix anything, you know."

Mary Ann blushed and looked out the window. "I'm just afraid, with Gertrude being such a strong sensitive, that if you develop your powers too, there won't be any room for me anymore." She blushed even more.

"That's a silly idea if I ever heard one," said Jim. "You'll be a part of the team as long as you want to be. Besides, who'll bake the cookies?"

Mary Ann's face didn't smile in response to Jim's teasing. "You've learned to bake pretty good cookies yourself," she said.

Jim gathered up the notes he had been working on and tapped them into tidiness. "Well then, let's look at the facts.

Gertrude hasn't any experience yet, so she can't assess what she sees as well as you can. It also helps if two people see the same thing. It gives the situation an aura of reality that it wouldn't have otherwise. I have more work than I can handle by myself right now, and you know yourself that I can only work on one case at a time, so the more help I have, the quicker the work gets done. I've had to rearrange that lecture series I was working on for UPEI to take on Connie's case because I can't do the two things at once, given that ghost hunting is mainly night work. So you see there are a lot of reasons why I need you, those not being the only ones."

Mary Ann took a deep breath and smiled her usual happy smile. "I'm relieved."

"You were really worried?" He watched the expressions come and go on Mary Ann's face.

"It was bothering me." She looked down and began to study her fingernails. They were chipped and broken as usual.

"Well, don't let it anymore. Besides," he said reaching over and patting her hand, "you add a lot to my life. I'd miss you if you weren't here."

Silence followed while Mary Ann thought this over.

Presently Jim said, "So what did you find out from Max Perry this morning?"

Mary Ann collected her thoughts. "It seems that Willie is a man of unpredictable temper. He's also of a nasty frame of mind about women, and anyone weaker than him is fair game." She related the morning's events.

"Hm." Jim frowned. "You say Max's married to the former Mrs. Poste? I wonder if we could get to talk to her?"

"He said that she never talks about Willie, that it's taken a lot of therapy to heal the damage he did to her. He seemed to want us to stay away from her, although he didn't expressly forbid it."

"Hm," said Jim again. "I wonder if I called her and put it to her that if it would help us to help Connie, would she talk a little about it? Even if she only confirms what we already know, it would be a help."

Mary Ann shrugged. "I guess it's worth a try at least. The worst she'll do is say no."

"I just hope it won't cause her any more trauma." He reached for the phone directory. "Perry … Perry." He slid his finger down the rows of P's. "Here it is." He picked up the receiver of his old rotary phone and began to dial. Presently he was talking to Marie Perry. "I'm sorry to bother you, Mrs. Perry, but I need to talk to you about something very serious concerning Connie Poste. Do you feel you could talk to me about this?"

Mrs. Perry was silent for so long that Jim began to think she wasn't there anymore. Finally she said softly, "What do you want to know?"

"Let me explain the situation, and then you can decide if you want to meet with me. There have been strange things happening out at the Poste residence and Mrs. Poste is scared out of her wits. I do investigations into psychic phenomena so she called me. In the course of my work it's necessary to do a full check of the house and its occupants as far back as we can get information. I understand that you were married to Mr. Poste at one time."

Mrs. Perry was silent again for a long moment. At last she said, "Yes, but what do you want from me?"

"If you would be willing to, for Connie's sake, I'd like to come by and meet with you to discuss Mr. Poste and his relationships with others, and the general ambiance of the house as well."

"My relationship with him too, I suppose."

"Only if you're willing to talk about it." Jim fiddled absently with the telephone cord, keeping his mental fingers crossed that she would consent.

Mrs. Perry sighed. "I'll tell you as much as I'm able to talk about, but come right now. If I stop to think about it, I'll probably change my mind."

"Thank you so much, Mrs. Perry. You'll be wonderfully helpful, I'm sure."

She sighed again. "My name's Marie."

"Wow!" Jim replaced the receiver. "I did it. I didn't think she'd agree to talk to me, but she did."

"When're you going?"

"Right now. She said she'd talk right now. Let's go!"

Soon they were ringing the doorbell at Max Perry's spacious home. It sat on two acres of parkland at the back of the college. A wing on either side of the brick front gave it the sense of a seagull taking flight. The whiteness of the wings added to the perception. A delicate clock melody sounded from within. Presently the peephole in the massive door opened briefly and then closed. The door opened a crack. "Yes?" asked a woman's voice.

"I have an appointment to see Marie Perry." Jim introduced himself and Mary Ann. The door opened wider.

"I'm Marie Perry," she said. "Come in." She turned and led the way into a bright airy living room. The paintings on the wall were bright splashes of colour. The walls were white behind them. Sheer curtains framed by dark red drapes surrounded each open window and billowed slightly in the summer breeze from the Hillsborough River. Between them a deep fireplace with a wide white mantle held imposing place. The unburnt logs in the fire bed were real.

"Please, make yourselves comfortable while I fetch another cup. I wasn't expecting two people." She left the room, a tall, elegant woman with midnight black hair drawn into a coil at the base of her neck, its single streak of white betraying her age.

"She's very beautiful," said Mary Ann when their hostess was out of hearing.

"She walks as if she could have been a dancer," said Jim. He followed her departure with his eyes, enjoying her grace of movement.

Marie returned with another cup and began pouring tea. "So how can I help you?" She passed a plate of tiny tea sandwiches to Mary Ann.

"I understand that you lived in the house on Everly Road for ten years," said Jim.

Marie nodded. "It was a spooky old house."

"Spooky?" Jim cocked his head. "In what way?"

"It creaked and groaned even on still nights. It was very eerie."

"Did you ever sense anything wrong with the house?"

"There was plenty wrong with it. What did you have in mind?"

"Well, for instance did you ever see anything strange there?"

"D'you mean like a ghost?"

"Yes, that's what I mean."

Marie shrugged. "I wouldn't be surprised if there were ghosts there. The place was very creepy, especially at night. But no, I never saw anything that might have been a ghost."

"When you say it was creepy, what exactly do you mean?" asked Mary Ann.

Marie jumped as if she had forgotten Mary Ann's presence. "Things kept disappearing. Nothing important, you understand, just little aggravating things."

"Like what?" asked Jim.

"Oh, I had a nice pair of sewing scissors, for example. I was working a piece of embroidery and I had them on the arm of my chair. One minute they were there, and the next they were gone. I turned the chair inside out looking for them but I never did find them. Of course not everything that disappeared was completely lost. Lots of times things would turn up in the next day or so, in a totally different place where you'd not expect to find them."

"Do you suppose Mr. Poste had anything to do with that?" Jim helped himself to another tiny sandwich.

"I thought so at first, but I asked him and he said I was crazy. He said that the next thing I'd be seeing things, so I never asked him again. I just looked for them myself and if I couldn't find them, I'd just get myself a new one of whatever it was."

"So Willie didn't deprive you of anything," said Mary Ann.

Again Marie looked startled to hear from Mary Ann. She laughed a small tinkling laugh and said, "I keep forgetting you're there, you sit so quietly. No, he tried once, but I threatened to destroy his reputation in the art world if he tried that on me, so he never denied me things as such." She sighed. "That was when I was still able to fight back."

"How do you mean that?" asked Jim. He watched the struggle of old emotions on her face.

For a long moment she moved uneasily in her chair and didn't answer. "How is this going to help Connie?" she finally asked.

"People leave behind vibrations on the ether. The older the house, the more vibrations there are. Also, the stronger the personality, the stronger the imprint."

"D'you mean that my vibrations are still on the air out there?"

"Exactly," said Jim. "So that's why it will be very helpful to us if you can bear to elaborate on your relationship with Mr. Poste."

"We didn't fight as such," said Marie. "At least not most of the time."

"But there was bad feeling between you?"

"All the time." Marie clutched her tea cup more tightly. She crossed her long elegant legs and forced herself to sit still.

"Did he ever beat you?" Mary Ann leaned forward in her chair.

"No, he never beat me." She sighed deeply and looked off into ancient space. "He didn't have to."

"How do you mean that?" asked Jim.

Marie stirred restlessly in her chair again. "There are other ways of destroying a person besides punching her out." Her knuckles were white with tension on her tea cup.

Jim frowned.

"Can you elaborate on that a little for us?" asked Mary Ann. "You needn't go into details too much, just an example would do."

"He was very good at name calling." Marie squirmed in her chair. Colour came and went in her complexion. "He has an unbelievably crude vocabulary, especially words that pertained to women's anatomy. Most of them I'd never heard before, but I knew instantly what they meant. Hair pulling was a favourite trick too. A little pressure on a lock of hair goes a long way to forcing a person to your will, and it doesn't show."

"Not on the outside, at least." Mary Ann's voice was soft.

"Did you ever think of having children?" Jim redirected the subject to try to ease the tension of the moment.

Marie looked at him sharply. "He didn't want them."

"Oh," said Jim. He changed the focus of his questions again. "Can you tell us about the house itself?"

"I don't really know very much. What do you want to know?"

"There seem to be psychic hot spots," said Mary Ann. "The library, the master bedroom, and the studio all seem to have a life of their own."

"Willie had the studio built to very specific requirements shortly after we moved in. It's very much his room. I was only allowed there on special invitation. He even cleaned it himself."

"Was that unusual?" asked Mary Ann.

Marie's face twisted into a small grimace. "It sure was. He was the sloppiest man I've ever had occasion to meet except in his studio."

"Was the library his room too?" asked Jim.

"Not really. Not like the studio was. I kept that dusted and vacuumed, although he had plenty to say if I didn't put things back in just the right order. How he ever knew where everything was to the last millimetre I'll never know."

"Did you have many arguments about it?" asked Mary Ann.

"We didn't argue." Marie sniffed. "He expounded, I listened and obeyed."

"What would happen if you didn't obey?" asked Mary Ann.

"He had ways." Marie stared into her tea cup remembering the past.

"What can you tell us about the master bedroom?" asked Jim.

"It was a very eerie room. I never liked to sleep there." Marie's hands tightened once more on her cup, her rings scraped harshly over its surface. She sat silently for a few minutes thinking. "So much unhappiness," she muttered, forgetting about Jim and Mary Ann. "My baby …" A tear slipped down her cheek. She sniffed and began rummaging in her pocket for a hanky, suddenly remembering her guests. "I'm sorry."

"You mentioned a baby?" asked Mary Ann.

Marie drew a long trembling breath. "I was pregnant once out there." She let the breath go slowly.

"Can you tell us about it?" asked Mary Ann. "But it's okay if you don't want to."

Marie straightened her slender shoulders. "It's all right,

I may as well tell you. It might even help Connie." She was silent for a long moment. "Willie didn't want children. He said that he'd never subject a child to a life like his was when he was growing up. It was about the only sane thing he ever said about relationships that I knew about." She leaned forward, her elbows on her knees. "At the same time, he didn't have any sense about adult relationships. He was very angry with me one night, and he more or less raped me. In those days there was no such thing as marital rape, you understand. I was never able to use the pill for birth control, we always used barrier methods, and that night he wouldn't wait. He twisted my arm behind my back and forced me into the bedroom and threw me on the bed. I was bleeding when he finished with me. I could hardly walk afterwards." She sat back in her chair and closed her eyes.

Presently she opened them again and continued her story. "Of course that would have to be the time of month that I could conceive, and I did. A few weeks later I suspected as much, and I didn't know what to do. I couldn't go to the doctor because Willie'd want to know why. I wasn't allowed to take the car without his permission, and he'd know if I was lying if I said I was going somewhere else. Besides, he never let me go anywhere, anyway."

"So what did you do?" asked Mary Ann.

"I waited a few more weeks. I had a very hard time concealing the morning sickness from him. He began to wonder why I wasn't eating much breakfast, and why I was so pale and listless. Eventually I started to show a little, and he put two and two together and figured it out." She closed her eyes again at the remembered pain.

"What did he do?" asked Jim.

"He was very angry." Her hands tightened on her empty tea cup once more. "He threw a tantrum as only Willie could. He grabbed me by the hair and forced me upstairs, then he pushed me down onto the bed and said, 'Pregnant? You want pregnant? I made this baby, I'll unmake it!' It was vicious. I lost the baby that night. I had to dispose of it myself. It was days after that before I could get out of bed." A sharp crack sounded. Marie looked down at her hands in surprise. The tea cup had broken in two.

Mary Ann reached out and took the pieces from her hands, and mopped up the drops of cold tea from her lap. "My dear, how could you stand it?" She took Marie's cold hands in her own and began to chafe some warmth back into them.

"I'd already lived with him for eight years by that time. I was used to that kind of treatment. It seemed almost normal to me. Well, not really normal," she amended, "but he had me convinced that I didn't deserve any better. I lived with him for two years after that, but nothing was ever the same again."

"Did he ever say anything about what he'd done?"

Marie shook her head. "He didn't come near me for about a week after that. He didn't even look in to see if I was dead or alive. He spent all his time up in his studio. I could hear him thumping around up there. Eventually I was able to get up and get myself cleaned up and make something to eat. He avoided me for several days after that, but soon he was back to his usual habits, carping and demanding and cursing at me for every little thing. Finally I just couldn't take it any more. I packed an overnight case and walked to town."

"But that's almost ten miles!"

"Well, I couldn't take the car." She shrugged. "He would have known I was going and tried to stop me."

"Where'd you go?"

"I came straight to Max and I've been here ever since.

I never even went back to get the rest of my things, not that I had that much anyway."

The front door clicked shut. "Max is home." Marie's face brightened. "I hope he won't be angry with me for talking about this."

Max strode into the room. "Hello, my dear, I see you have vis …" He turned to see who the visitors were. "I thought I told you not to bother my wife! How dare you go against my wishes!"

Marie jumped up from her chair and took Max by the hand. "Hush, darling, it's alright. There's no harm done, and it may help poor Connie."

Max calmed himself. "I'm sorry you had to be disturbed by these people. I told them …"

"You told me that if Marie wanted to talk about this it was up to her," said Mary Ann. "The only thing you said against it was that she never talked about it and probably wouldn't want to now."

"And I did want to talk about it," said Marie. "Well, not exactly want to, but it was for Connie's sake."

"Well, I hope this hasn't done any harm." Max's

expression was grim. "I sure don't want you to slide back into misery."

"I won't, I promise," said Marie. "Actually I feel better now that I've told someone who can do something about the situation out there. I've worried about Connie such a lot over the years. We never hear from her, and I've been very afraid that the same thing was happening to her."

"We don't know that it is," said Jim. "She's very unhappy, I do know that, but she won't say why. I think it may have a lot to do with the strange things that have been happening at the house. If we can only solve that problem maybe it will ease her worries. She's also quite worried about Mr. Poste's condition. I guess he's not doing very well."

"That fall was the strangest thing," said Marie. "Willie was always as sure-footed as a cat, and just as silent when he wanted to be. He'd paint those big murals up on catwalks only one plank wide and never miss a step. It's a very strange thing that he'd fall downstairs." She sighed. "Maybe age is catching up with him."

Max began to pace. "More likely she pushed him, if she had any sense. There'd be no one there to ever say that she did it, and he'd certainly deserve it too."

"Well," said Jim, "whatever went on out there between those two we'll likely never know unless she tells us. In the meantime we have a lot of work to do to get the ghosties straightened out." He rose from his chair, and Mary Ann followed him.

"Thank you for telling us this, Marie, I know it must have been very painful for you. I'm sorry to have upset you, Max, but it was in a good cause." Mary Ann turned to leave.

"I sincerely hope so," said Max.

Marie showed them to the door. "The baby was a little girl," she said softly. "I've always called her Sarah in my mind."

"Catch him!" cried Lucy, as the two spirits gave chase to Willie who had escaped their guard. He had behaved quite nicely during the review of his life, but had erupted into his previous behaviour toward the end. It had begun as he watched the film. His first response had been, "Why that's me!" After that he'd viewed the whole thing without saying a word, merely sinking deeper and deeper into his chair as each incident was recalled and displayed before him in inglorious living colour. At first he only whimpered, then he began to cry out, finally he began to babble incoherently. At this point he jumped to his feet and ran out the door.

"Don't let him get through the gate," cried Lucy. Molly floated between him and the fence and managed to steer him away down the hill. He ran blindly through bushes and over streams leaving bits of his attire decorating the landscape as he went.

"We'd better catch him before he's completely nude," shouted Molly, gleefully in pursuit of the pudgy Willie. "That'd be a sight for the Sunday papers!"

"Oh, I wish Larry was here." Lucy zoomed as fast as she could after Molly and Willie.

"Are you girls in trouble again?" Larry barrelled past them and planted himself firmly in Willie's path bringing him to a sudden stop. Willie fell to the ground in a grubby heap, curled himself into a ball and lay there whimpering and sighing.

"Humph!" said Molly. "That was quite a display. He's completely out of control again." She glared down at the unpleasant pile at her feet.

"Oh, dear," said Lucy, "I do hope this doesn't happen

often. What do we do with him now?" She looked to Larry.

"Drag him back to the centre and put him to bed. He'll sleep it off by morning." He pushed Willie gently in the ribs with the toe of his shoe. "C'mon Willie, up and at 'em. We're not going to do all the work this time." Willie groaned a hideous groan and rolled onto his knees. Larry grabbed him by the arm and told Molly to do likewise. Together they heaved the nearly comatose Willie to his feet and started out of the valley with him.

CHAPTER SIX

Jim spent the next morning at the Confederation Centre library and the court house searching out the previous owners of the Poste house. Without the deeds in hand his search was only partially successful. He managed to trace the family who had lived there immediately before Willie. The Garretts now lived out on the Spruce Road behind Charlottetown. It had been a busy road between farms in the old days but now it was a shabby rundown lane with grass growing in the middle and the trees overshadowing it where there used to be open fields. It was much deplored and much debated by the city council, some wanting to turn the land into an upscale housing development and some arguing that it was more money than they had to spend on such a project. So the area remained undeveloped and unused except by the few eccentric residents who called it home.

I think Betsy might like a car ride this afternoon, thought Jim, not really allowing himself to think about what taking Betsy along might imply about his attitude toward the area.

After lunch he left a note to the others in plain view on the kitchen table, and he and Betsy piled into the tiny car and drove off in search of a garrulous Garrett. He was in luck. The first house he stopped at up the rutted lane housed Georgie and Gus Garrett, children of the previous owners.

He left Betsy in the car with the window wide open and the admonition to stay, and made his way through the broken gate and up the weedy path to the front door. He pounded on the cracked and peeling panels, eliciting a shout from the other side. In a moment the door was wrenched open, revealing a being of immense proportions. Jim could hardly take in what had presented itself to his eyes.

"What d'ya want?" enquired the being in a gruff voice. It was engulfed in a voluminous faded plaid shirt and baggy torn jeans. It appeared to be neither male nor female.

Jim found his voice, and though unsure of the sex of

this being, managed to say in normal tones, "I'm looking for a Gus or Georgie Garrett."

"I'm Gus. What d'ya want?"

"Information about the history of a house on the Everly Road," said Jim.

"I used ta live out there," said Gus, brushing a ragged lock of greying hair out of his eyes with an immense fist. "I was brought up there. C'm in, I'm gettin' bread ready for the pans, and it can't wait." The door opened wider.

Jim stepped over the threshold into the cluttered gloom. "My name is Jim MacDonald," he said offering his hand.

"The ghost hunter?" Gus engulfed Jim's large hand in a surprisingly soft one. "I heard about you. You cleared out my cousin's place up west. Awful queer things went on over there before you 'exercised' it. Whatcha want to know about the place at Everly?" He led the way to the kitchen. "Have a seat, I'll talk while I work. Georgie'll be home soon. She works cleanin' houses in town."

"Oh," said Jim, "I didn't know that." To himself he thought, so Georgie's a female.

"Yep, Georgie works there and I works here." Gus tipped the large bowl of bread out on the table and began to knead vigorously. Jim watched in fascination, slowly becoming aware that there were large and pendulous breasts moving under the man's flannel shirt in rhythm with the kneading of the bread.

So this one's a female too, he thought, staring in semi-horror at the spectacle.

"So, whatcha want to know about Everly?"

Jim recalled his manners and tried to pretend that he hadn't been staring. He shifted his gaze to the chaos of the kitchen taking in the dusty green bead board walls, the greasy wood stove with its broken oven door propped shut with a stout stick of wood. "You say you were brought up there. How long did you live there?" His eyes followed the stacks of used dishes on the counter to avoid the horrid fascination of the kneading figure in front of him.

"Yep, me 'n my brothers and sisters, we all lived there, all twelve of us, and Maw and Paw. They lived there about thirty years, Maw and Paw did. 'Til they died. Spooky old place."

"D'you know who owned it before you?" He glanced at Gus then away, to study the collection of wood chips and bark decorating the floor, a thicker layer around the stove and wood box.

"Nope. It'd been in the family for three generations by that time. Great-granpaw may have built it for all I know."

The rhythmic kneading continued. The massive breasts swayed with it. Jim had difficulty keeping his eyes on other things. He cleared his throat and began to take in the pressed tin ceiling and the faded curtains hanging awry at the windows. Streamers of dust hung off every projection and gave the atmosphere a misty density. "You say it was spooky?"

"Yep, 'specially at night. That old house would creak and groan like a living thing. Once us kids got in bed at night we was scared to get out again, in case the ghosts got us." She chuckled a rich, rumbling chuckle as massive as herself. "Maw and Paw used to brag about how good we was to go to bed. They never knew the reason why."

"How'd your folks get along?" Jim shifted his massive body on the kitchen chair. It creaked and snapped. Jim sat still again. He tried moving his legs into a more comfortable position. Minimal creaking from the chair changed his mind and he stayed where he was.

"Pretty good. Why?"

"Well, old houses tend to hold the atmosphere of the people who lived in them. That's why ghosts can show up in them."

The hands stopped kneading. "What d'ya mean? The place is haunted?"

"In common terms, it would seem so," said Jim.

"I told that Georgie so! I just told her so, and she wouldn't believe me." She returned to her kneading for a few more strokes.

"What made you think it was haunted?"

Gus began cutting the bread into loaf-sized pieces. "I saw somethin' one night. I woke up in the middle of the night and there was a figure all in white standing by the foot of the bed. I covered up my head real quick and didn't come up for air until mornin'. I never told no one neither."

"Why not?" Jim glanced at Gus to discover that the scenery had stopped moving. He relaxed. The chair creaked again.

"Didn't want them to think I was crazy. B'sides, things was always disappearin' around there."

"Oh?" said Jim. "What sorts of things?"

"Yeah, just little stuff. Maw'd always blame it on us kids."

She began greasing blackened loaf pans. "We knew better."

"How would you know better?"

"We'd ask amongst ourselves."

"Could one of you have been playing a prank on the others?"

"You mean lie about it? No way. We was always too scared of the ghost. B'sides, if one of us was ever caught lyin' about it, the rest of us would've pounded the stuffin' out of him and we all knew it. We was too scared!" She plopped a loaf of bread dough forcefully into the pan to emphasize her point.

"D'you know if anyone besides you ever saw anything out of the ordinary in the house?"

"No, we didn't like to talk about it." Gus cut another lump of loaf-sized dough and began to shape it.

"Hm," said Jim, "it seems that you all really thought there was something there. How'd your folks get along?"

"I told ya already, pretty good."

"No fights or major disagreements?"

"They fought all the time. Isn't that what most people do?"

Jim's lips had a hard time keeping a straight line. "No,

many people hardly ever fight."

"Well, there's nothin' like a good free-for-all to clear the air and keep the lines open, Maw always said," said Gus. She plunked the loaf into the pan. "Maw and Paw was always at it, and when they wasn't fightin' they was lovin'. That's why there's twelve of us."

"What would they fight about?"

"Everythin'. It didn't take much." She began to squeeze small blobs of dough through her enormous fists to make cloverleaf rolls with the remainder of the dough. "Sometimes it was just about how one would look at the other."

"Did you children fight?"

"Us kids? No, not so's you notice, anyway. We always played by ourselves so there was no one to fight with. The only ones we'd ever fight with were the neighbour kids. They'd leave themselves wide open for it all the time."

"Do you remember if your folks ever fought about anything serious?"

"No, they never did, but Gran' and Granpaw used to have rousers. They was worse than Maw and Paw ever thought o' bein'. They'd come to blows when it got bad enough. Us kids would always duck before it got that bad though. You'd never know when you'd get a cuff on the side of the head intended for one or the other of those two. That's a long time ago now."

"They lived with you, then?"

Gus shrugged. "Off and on. Maw'd get sick of the fightin' and throw them out every now and then. They'd stay away for a few weeks and then be right back." She finished arranging the bread pans in the oven and propped the door shut with the stick of wood.

"D'you know what their fighting was about?"

"As far as I could figure, it hadn't much to do with what was going on right then. When I got old enough to ask questions and listen in and understand adult conversations, I found out that Gran' had been in the family way and had to get married, only Granpaw wasn't the father, an' he didn't find out about it 'til after the weddin'." She chuckled her enormous chuckle again. "'Course he must have been doin' somethin' for him to think it was his in the first place!"

Jim permitted himself a smile. "So you think that their fighting stemmed from that?"

Gus shrugged. "Maybe not all of it. There was the time Granpaw caught Gran' in the hayloft with the neighbour's hired man. He wasn't pleased about that. She was in her sixties then. She could hardly climb the ladder to the loft, her knees was so bad with 'artheritis' by then. But she made it once at least." Gus chuckled again. "At least she didn't have to worry about lyin' about offspring that time."

"So there were a variety of aggravations in your grand-father's life."

"All the time," said Gus. "Gran mostly deserved what she got." She rose from her chair and stirred up the fire. "Can I offer you a cuppa tea?"

"That would be just fine, thank you," said Jim. He thought to himself, I might not survive the experience but I can't refuse. The temperature from the stove makes the place like a sauna. Between the heat and the tea I may go up in smoke, if the dirt doesn't get me first, he thought. He watched his hostess blowing the dust out of a china cup.

"D'you know of anyone who might have known your family before you were born?"

"D'you mean like the greats?"

"Yes, I wonder if anyone would know about the greats."

"Oh, I don't think so, not now. They'd all be dead." Gus sipped her tea with a plump pinkie raised. She searched the corners of her mind for a few minutes. "'Course there's old Jobie down at the nursin' home in town. If he's still in his right mind he might remember them. He must be about a 'hunnerd' by now. He was only a boy them times."

Jim drained his tea cup. "Well, you've been a tremendous help, Gus. May I come back and visit again if I need help?"

"Hell, you can come anytime you've a mind to. I'm always glad o' the company."

Jim called a meeting at his house that evening.

"I've had a very profitable afternoon," said Jim. He organized his notes into greater coherency. "I had a visit with Gus Garrett. She had all kinds of interesting things to tell me about the Poste house."

"D'you mean Gus Garrett on the Spruce Road?" asked Mary Ann from the rocker. "I always thought Gus was a man. You couldn't have gotten me to go up there alone if you'd paid me." She began to rock more vigorously.

"Well, she's a she, although it's very hard to tell. So's Georgie for that matter. Besides I took Betsy along for company." He made a note in the margin then looked up. "By the way, Gertrude, do you remember having a patient by the name of Jobie at the nursing home when you worked there?"

Gertrude set down her mug and thought for a moment. "If you mean Joe B. Pringle, I do. He's about a hundred years old, and as sharp as a tack. He knows everything about everyone. I didn't know he was called Jobie though."

Jim shrugged. "According to Gus, he is. She said if he was in his right mind he'd probably remember her great-grandparents."

"So where does Gus fit into all this?" Don poured himself some more coffee.

"She and her family used to live in Willie's house. In fact several generations of Garretts grew up there. She says the place is haunted." Jim rose from his place to stir the fire.

"Well, that would certainly explain all the strange happenings out there these days," said Mary Ann. "I'd like to go out and try again to get a fix on the spirits that might be causing all this."

"I'm going back tonight to set up some human traps," said Jim. "Want to come along? It'll be an all-nighter."

Mary Ann's eyes sparkled. "You bet! Why don't we all

go? Trudy's never been on a stake-out before."

Don frowned. "I can't. Tomorrow's a working day for me." He took a deep breath as an expression of worry crossed his face. "But you go if you want to, Gertrude," he said.

Gertrude jumped out of her chair and threw her arms around him. "Oh, thank you, darling. Are you sure?"

Don smiled at her, taking in her eager face. "No, I'm not, but I'm going to trust Jim to look after you." He glared at Jim. "He'd better too!"

Jim laughed. "I will. I promise."

"Oh, goody! Then it's settled. I'm so excited."

Jim, Mary Ann, Gertrude, and Betsy arrived at Willie's house at eleven o'clock that evening. Jim had made arrangements with Connie for them to have free run of the house for the night. As usual, on their arrival, the house was lighted from ceiling to cellar, although for once it was fairly quiet. They found Connie in the greenhouse.

"How's Willie tonight?" asked Jim as he came through the door.

Connie sighed. "There's been no change. The doctors are beginning to give up hope of him ever being normal again." She sighed again. "Poor Willie, I wouldn't wish this on my worst enemy."

"It is too bad," said Jim. "A vital, able man like that." He shifted his bag of ghost hunting equipment to his other hand. "Has the house been quiet this evening?"

Connie played with her braid. "Fairly quiet. Just a few thumps and an occasional crash. Nothing like it has been." She sighed again. "I wish it would stop."

"I'm sure you do, and that's what we're here for, so if you don't mind, we'll just get on with our work. Would you like Betsy to stay here with you?"

Connie smiled, the first real smile they'd seen from her. "That would be wonderful. Maybe I should get a dog again. I had one once you know." Her face drooped. "Sandy was my friend."

"They're grand company." Jim turned to go through the house. "We'll see you in the morning."

"There's coffee in the kitchen, I made a big pot," called Connie.

They climbed the stairs to the third floor. "What

happens first?" asked Gertrude.

"First I set up a camera on a tripod with a trip-wire, so that if anything solid disturbs it, it'll go off. Then I run a string of fine sewing thread across the windows, and around the walls to make sure there's no way that anyone can get in without us knowing about it. Then I dust the whole floor lightly with flour to show up any footprints that might be made by a human prankster. Then we make ourselves comfortable on the landing and while away the night."

"With the lights on?" asked Gertrude.

"Any way you like it." Jim laughed. "You're not scared, are you?" He opened the door to the studio and switched on the light. Everything appeared much the same as before. A few things on the workbench were disarranged, but the room was essentially quite neat.

"A little," said Gertrude, "after all, I've never done this before."

"You'll get used to it in no time," said Mary Ann. "There's really not much to be scared of." She took the spool of thread from Jim and climbed up on the workbench. "You could climb up here with me and help me stick this to the window frames. It goes faster with two."

Gertrude hitched herself up beside Mary Ann.

Jim busied himself setting up the camera. It clicked and whirred several times before he was satisfied with it. He placed thermometers at various points about the room and hooked them up to their recording device. A machine for measuring power surges was set up, and at last all was ready except to dust the floor with flour.

"Here," he said, "you might as well learn how to do this without disturbing what you've already done." He demonstrated the amount and the method of sprinkling, then handed the can to Gertrude.

She completed the task and then asked, "What happens now?"

"I'm going to find us some chairs and some of that coffee and we wait." Jim ushered the girls out of the room, turned off the light and closed the door. "I want you and Mary Ann to stay right here on the landing while I do that. We want to keep an eye on the door during the night." He turned and trudged down the steps.

Gertrude and Mary Ann perched themselves on the landing steps and waited for Jim to return. They were chatting between themselves when Mary Ann's eyes grew round with horror. "Is that what I think it is?" She pointed at the newel post.

"What? Where?" Gertrude tried to follow the direction of Mary Ann's finger.

"Right there! On the corner of the post."

"Oh, yuck! I think it is." Gertrude inspected the spot more closely.

"What is?" Jim returned with a chair.

"A bit of Wee Willie still clinging to the post," said Mary Ann.

"That may be the source of the disturbance," said Jim. "I'll bring back a rag and clean it off, then we'll see how the night progresses." He trudged back down stairs again.

"What did he mean by that?" asked Gertrude.

Mary Ann shrugged. "He just meant that sometimes if a piece of remains is left behind, the spirit goes to a lot of trouble trying to clean up after itself so to speak."

"But Willy's not dead."

A thump sounded inside the room. Mary Ann shivered. "I wish Jim would get back here."

Presently Jim returned with another chair and a wet rag. "I asked Connie about this when I was downstairs. She said that she'd already cleaned the stairs." He scrubbed the post.

"I guess she must have missed some," said Mary Ann.

Jim made another trip downstairs. The studio began to get noisy again. Glass broke and something upset with a crash. Jim returned with a third chair. "I'm sorry they're only straight chairs," he said, "but they're the only ones that would fit on the landing all at once." Another crash resounded inside the room.

"Do you mind if I go down and get the coffee?" asked Mary Ann.

"What's the matter Mary Ann, too noisy for you here?" Jim laughed his rumbling laugh.

"Of course not. I just want a little break, that's all." She hurried down the stairs.

"You're not afraid, are you, Trudy?" asked Jim.

"Not really," said Gertrude. "I'd just love to know what's going on in that room. It would ease my mind considerably." Something jingly hit the wall above their heads, and cascaded to the floor. Gertrude paled. "I'm just glad it's not my house." She held her ground.

"Spoken like a true ghost hunter." Jim arranged the chairs in a conversational grouping on the landing. "Actually, there's probably not much going on in there anyway. Just a lot of noise."

Another crash resounded from the studio just as Mary Ann returned with a tray of coffee. "Cleaning up after Wee Willie doesn't seem to have made much difference." She set the tray down on the step.

The night passed slowly. The noise in the room above them continued in a sporadic fashion, as did the conversation on the landing. Toward morning the collective yawns grew wider as they each fought to stay awake. At birdsong the noises finally ceased and at sunrise Jim roused himself from his drowsy state.

"Wakey, wakey, my fearless fellow ghost hunters. Let's go see what the night has brought us."

Mary Ann and Gertrude yawned and stretched, then rose stiffly to their feet to trudge up the stairs after Jim. He opened the studio door very carefully. The work bench was a shambles of overturned paint cans and brushes, turpentine dripped between the wooden planks onto the floor, tubes of paint lay squashed among the mess. The camera stood where Jim had left it, the trip wire untripped. The morning sun poured through the windows shining off the sewing thread that sealed them. The carpet of flour still covered the floor in pristine whiteness except where the turpentine had dripped through from the bench. No other mark marred its perfection.

"Well," said Jim, "unless the guy can fly, no one's been in here since last night."

"So we really do have ghosts?" said Gertrude.

"It would seem so." Jim checked his other equipment. "These graphs show two major power surges during the night at just about the time that it got noisy in here. The temperature dropped significantly then too. Now the trick is to discover who's behind it."

"Will that be very difficult?" asked Gertrude.

"I hope not," said Jim. "I want to go and interview Jobie at the nursing home today and hear what he has to say about this place. I'll do that this afternoon." He went into the studio to retrieve his camera. "I'll need to take the film in to have it developed too. The sooner we know what went on here last night, the sooner we'll know what we're dealing with."

He picked up the camera bag and tripod, and trudged downstairs with it, leaving white footprints behind. Mary

Ann and Gertrude trudged after him lugging the rest of the equipment. They went through the greenhouse to retrieve Betsy who greeted them with a happy woof and a big doggie yawn. Connie wakened with a start.

"Sorry to frighten you," said Jim, "We're finished here for this evening. We were just leaving."

Connie sat up among her welter of blankets looking more refreshed and younger than they'd ever seen her. "That's the best sleep I've had in ages. Your Betsy's real good company."

"It probably helped having people in the house too," said Gertrude. "I know I never slept well when I was living alone."

Anxiety crossed Connie's face again. "What did you discover?" she asked.

"It's nothing physical that I can determine. I have a few more things I'd like to do up there, and some more people to interview before I say definitely what it is. After I discover what's doing it I'll know better how to deal with it. By the way, you'll probably want to vacuum up there today, we made kind of a mess."

Connie looked more alarmed than ever. "I don't know

if I can go up there by myself."

"Of course you can. There's nothing up there to hurt you. Ghosts can't hurt anything in the physical unless they start throwing things."

"What do I do if they do that?"

Jim grinned. "You duck of course. Now I don't want you to worry about all this. As long as you stay away from the studio at night you'll be all right. We'll probably be back tomorrow evening."

"Not tonight?"

Jim shook his head. "I have to sleep sometime, and I have some research to do about this place this afternoon."

They took their leave against Connie's pleas to stay for breakfast, and couldn't they come back tonight even just for a few minutes.

"She's one scared lady," said Jim.

CHAPTER SEVEN

Jim pulled into the parking lot of the Sunset Manor that afternoon. "It's hard to believe that Gertrude worked nights here," he mused. He sat looking at the ancient building with all its gables and peeling paint. "The place is spooky enough on its own, without having Molly and Lucy paying their questionable visits."

The building had once been a large private residence in the days when servants weren't expensive to keep. Its colonnaded front porch on its red sandstone supports sagged ever so slightly now, the windows had shrunk a little in their frames and rattled when the wind blew hard enough, the paintwork around them had been kept up but was beginning to peel just around the edges. Inside, the dark floor tiles curled in various places along the wall, but nowhere dangerously. The walls had been painted bright colours in an attempt to lighten the darkness of the interior without much success. Over the years a thousand wheelchairs had scarred the woodwork around the doors. The whole place reeked of disinfectant and old age. It was spotless.

Jim enquired after Jobie and was ushered into a room at the end of the hall. A small bony pile under the blankets and a grizzled head on the single pillow were the only signs that anyone occupied the bed, so thin had Jobie become in his declining years. He was just waking up from his afternoon nap.

"Good afternoon, Mr. Pringle," said Jim, extending his hand in greeting.

Jobie peered almost sightlessly in Jim's direction, searching the gloom to put form to the shadows of his failing vision.

"Eh?" cackled Jobie. "Gimme my glasses so I can hear ya." He yawned a cavernous, toothless yawn, his moist red gums shining wetly in the small ray of sunshine that crept around the edge of the blind.

Jim searched the bedside stand and found a pair of glasses with a hearing aid attached to each bow, and handed them to Jobie.

Jobie adjusted them on his beaky nose and fumbled the hearing aids into place. "Now, what's that ya said?" He peered in Jim's direction.

Jim held out his hand again and introduced himself. The blankets fluttered briefly and a skinny moist hand was thrust into his, its grip still strong.

"How'd ya do? I'm pleased to meet ya. Don't get many visitors these days, I outlived them all ya know. Put up that blind will ya, we need some light on the subject."

Jim pulled up the blind and a flood of sunshine entered the room.

"That's better," said Jobie. "Now I can see ya. What can I do for ya?"

"I need some information, Mr. Pringle," said Jim.

"Call me Jobie. Nobody calls me Mr. Pringle anymore. What d'ya want to know?"

"D'you remember the Garretts out on the Everly Road?"

Jobie cackled with laughter. "Which generation?" he wheezed.

"Anything you can tell me will be helpful," said Jim, "but I'm most interested in the earliest ones."

Jobie thought for a moment. "That'd be old George

and Gussie. Had thirteen kids. An awful wild bunch." He cackled again. "They used to get up to the worst shenanigans, them kids. They was older than me, but I 'member them, and the old people too. That was a long time ago." He fell silent for a few minutes, lost in the years.

Jim waited for Jobie. After a few minutes he prompted him. "They were a wild bunch, were they?"

"Oh, yes. The old man and the old woman had no control of them. They'd be out 'til all hours, ate when they wanted to, went to bed when they wanted to, and went to school when they wanted to." Jobie cackled again. "'Cept when the truant officer got after them. They'd all be playin' in the barnyard and they'd see the truant officer's dust comin' up the lane and they'd be gone. Their maw and paw couldn't find them anywhere. They'd come home again when they'd get hungry and when they was sure that the truant officer'd left."

"Was it them who built the house out there then?"

"Eh? What'd ya say?" Jobie had been lost in another time.

Jim leaned closer to Jobie. "I was wondering if they were the ones that had built the house out there."

"Oh, yes. T'was, indeed," said Jobie. "It was much

smaller then, of course. It's been added onto over the years. The old people, Gussie and George, you know, just built the front part. There was two main rooms, a sleeping loft, and a kitchen and porch combined. For all his harem-scarum ways, George was good carpenter. He was lazy though, an' 'ud only work when he felt like it. He built the front part of the house intendin' to add to it when they could afford it. 'Course they never could."

"Do you remember it being built?"

Jobie processed the question for a moment. "No, that was before my time, though I did hear stories about how they come by the lumber to build it." His eyes took on the knowing look of the practised gossip.

Jim smiled and tried not to look too eager. "And how was that?"

"When they was building the city hall. Not the one they have now but the first one. They kept losin' lumber. For awhile it was almost every night. They couldn't catch who was doin' it, though they had their suspicions. Charlie Preston said, 'I'll fix them.' He had a dog that was awful cross. It'd guard anythin' he'd set him to guardin', and you couldn't get near it. The dog was real quiet, too. Ya'd never hear him 'til it was too late." Jobie gave a cackle of delighted laughter. "Well, Charlie set the dog to guardin' the buildin' site without tellin' anyone, and that same night along about midnight, there was an awful racket started there. People yellin', the dog snarlin' and barkin', and then an awful shriek, then silence except for some serious moanin'. Lights came on all around, but by the time anyone got there, no one was there, 'cept the dog, of course. He was lickin' his chops an' there was blood on his muzzle. Charlie said, 'Now we'll see who comes for treatment of dog bite.' But no one ever did."

"How'd they find out it was the Garretts?"

"Well, the next day was Sunday, and no matter what the men-folk was up to durin' the week old Gussie'd make them go to church on Sunday. That Sunday George had an awful hard time sittin' still."

"That wasn't much proof," said Jim.

"No, not by itself, t'wasn't, but Charlie put two and two together, and came up pretty close to four when he greeted George right friendly with a smack on the rump! I found out for sure the story was likely true after he died. They called me to lay him out for them, I was workin' for the undertaker then ya know, and I seen them scars on old George's rump. Two long grooves with a dimple in the middle that the dog got."

Jim chuckled. "It's no wonder he had trouble sitting still." They were silent for a moment.

Jim broke the silence. "Was there ever any trouble out there?"

"Trouble! Humph! There was always trouble of one kind or another, all of it their own makin,'" said Jobie. "What kind was ya thinkin' of?"

"Well, for instance, did they fight a lot among themselves?"

"Fight? They was always fightin'! Them kids was bad for fightin' amongst themselves, and the old man and the old woman weren't far behind them. They fought like cats and dogs amongst themselves all right, but let anyone challenge one of them and ya'd have the whole clan down on ya at the same time. They was vicious fighters all right. They'd egg each other on, ya know. They was awful hard on one of the boys. He wasn't quite right in the head. Simple, ya know. They say the old grandmother dropped him on his head when he was a baby. So if they didn't have somethin' to fight about for real, they'd pick on him. They'd set him up, too, for all kinds of pranks, and the poor fellow'd always go along. He'd forget, ya know." Jobie's wrinkled face suddenly split into a toothless grin.

"I 'member one time. He used to like to chew 'tabacca,' and one Sunday just before church the other boys offered it to him. He took a big bite 'cause he never got it very often and went in to church. Well, he wasn't there very long when he discovered that he had nowhere to spit, and the minister was just gettin' launched into the service. He looked around for somewhere but couldn't decide what to do, him bein' simple, ya know. In the meantime his mouth was gettin' fuller and fuller, and the poor feller was in distress. In them days the men used to leave their Sunday hats on the back pew rather than have to hold them all through the service. One of the other boys offered him Deacon Bates' hat and told him it was all right to spit in it, that they could wash it out afterwards. Well, by the end of the service the hat was gettin' to be about half full of spit an' 'tabacca' juice. It was lined with dark material an' ya couldn't really see anythin' in it. Anyway, the deacon came down the aisle after the service and picked up his hat and clamped it on his head as soon as he got out the door." Jobie was laughing so hard the tears were running down his wrinkled cheeks. "Hee, hee, hee," he cackled, "He was some mad deacon!"

Jim laughed too. "What happened then?"

"Oh, nothin' much. They couldn't do very much to Lyman, him bein' simple and all. The other boys ran, of course, and when they caught up with them they were innocent of any mischief. Butter wouldn't-a melted in their mouths. The Deacon had to get a new hat, and it was right after that that they put holders under each pew for the men's hats. I think the Deacon donated the money."

"So, they were a pretty rowdy bunch out there," said Jim.

"Yes, and each generation got worse. Seems as if every time they'd add to the house the fights'd get worse. More vicious, ya know. Old Gussie and George, when they'd fight there was always some humour in it, but when they died they left the place to the oldest son and his wife. She was a Watson from over on the Mill Road by Victoria Cross. Them Watson's was great fighters too, ya know. Anyway, like I said, the fights got worse. Real nasty like, an' unforgivin'. The next generation was the same. I heard that Mamie, she'd be the wife of the oldest grandson, took the butcher knife one day and threatened to stab Henry, I think his name was Henry. She was hateful, that one."

"So there's been lots of fights and bad feeling in that house over the years." Jim shifted his bulk in the chair. This one was sturdy metal and didn't creak.

"Ya could say that," said Jobie.

"Was there ever any talk about the place being haunted?"

"People didn't hardly ever go there, so there was never much to say about the place unless one of the family said somethin'. Of course, it wouldn't s'prise me a bit if t'was haunted," said Jobie.

"Why's that?" asked Jim.

"Well, poor Lyman hanged himself in the attic."

"Did he now," said Jim. "Did they ever say why?"

"The kids had put him up to one trick too many and he finally had enough I guess. Anyway, he disappeared right before Christmas, he was always doin' that, ya know. He'd go off for days at a time, no one knew where, then he'd come back again. This time he didn't. They didn't look very hard for him 'cause they thought he'd come back on his own. When he didn't they just figured he'd gone for good, and forgot about him. They found his body in the spring when the sun got hot on the roof and he thawed. I guess he was pretty ripe by that time, only the cold kept him from smellin' before that. I was just a young feller then, but I 'member that." Jobie was silent for so long this time that Jim thought he'd gone to sleep and stood up to creep out without disturbing him. Suddenly Jobie opened his eyes and peered keenly at Jim. "What's your interest in all this?" he asked.

Jim sat down again. "There've been some disturbances up there that are difficult to explain, and I'm investigating them."

"Haunted, huh?' Jobie's beady eyes sparkled. "That's interestin'. You'll have to come back and tell me how it comes out."

Jim got up to leave. "You've been an enormous help, Jobie. Thank you. D'you mind if I come back if I need to?"

"Why sure, young feller, come any time you've a mind to. I'm not goin' any place. Ya'd be welcome any time."

Jim turned toward the door. "An' bring me some 'tabacca,' will ya?" said Jobie. "Please?"

❖

The summer sun slanted low through the windows as the little group of spook sleuths gathered at Jim's house that evening to summarize their findings and discuss their next move. Don and Gertrude were the first to arrive as usual. They sat around the big kitchen table sipping the inevitable cup of coffee while Jim bustled about taking cookies out of the oven.

"Why do you wear a ruffled apron?" asked Gertrude.

"It's a tradition." Jim looked down at the incongruous ruffles covering the bulk of his large person. "It was my grandmother's, and when I was a little boy she taught me how to make chocolate chip cookies wearing an apron like this. When she died, I fell heir to a large box of her things and this was among them. Until I moved in here ten years ago I hadn't done any more cooking or baking, so when Mary Ann saw my lack of culinary expertise, and the sad state of my nutrition, she took me in hand and gave me some elementary cooking and baking lessons. I was terribly messy when I started and I needed an apron of some sort, so I pulled this out of the box and I've been wearing it ever since." He put the last of the cookies on the racks to cool just as Mary Ann walked in bearing a cake saver.

"You had the baking bug too, did you? I should have known. I've been feeling your vibes since supper time. I should have paid attention." She set the cake saver down on the table and uncovered a creation in orange and coconut.

"Good grief!" exclaimed Gertrude, "we'll all be as fat as little piggies if we keep eating like this. I've already had to take up aerobics for damage control!"

"Oh, but it's so good." Mary Ann gave a warm chuckle. "A little piece won't hurt."

"Will you two stop obsessing about food and just enjoy it," said Don.

"Yes," said Jim, "just stop obsessing and get down to the serious business of eating." He poured Mary Ann some coffee. "I had a very interesting afternoon," he said. He pulled off his apron, sat down and changed the subject.

"You visited with Jobie," said Gertrude. "How was he?"

Jim shook his head in amazement. "He's as alert as a young man, and full to the brim with ancient gossip, and I mean really ancient stuff. He told me all about the Garretts right back to the building of the house."

"He was always full of news when I worked there, but I never seemed to have time for him. I always had something else to do," said Gertrude. "He liked to know all about everyone. So what did he say about them?"

"He didn't remember the building of the house, that was before his time he said, but he had plenty of stories about it, and delighted in every one. I guess the place had been the scene of some fierce family battles over the years in every generation."

Mary Ann looked thoughtfully at her cookie and said, "That could explain the psychic chaos there."

"He also said that one of them hanged himself in the attic during the winter and they didn't find him until spring."

"I think that's more likely it than the fights," said Gertrude. "The studio's in the attic and the beams are all bare."

"If it's that specific," said Mary Ann thoughtfully, "why are we not able to get a fix on it better than we have? And where are Molly and Lucy these days?"

Gertrude sat for a few minutes pondering the psychic facts. "You're right," she said, "I don't think the fights and the hanging are the whole story. If it were that specific we'd be able to sort it out more readily, and Molly and Lucy would be doing some heavy interfering. Molly especially.

I wonder where they are? When they were haunting me, they were here every time I turned around, and usually at the worst possible moment. I even called Molly the other day when I was in trance and she didn't answer. That was really unusual."

"Well, wherever they are," said Jim, "they're probably up to something. I can't imagine that Molly keeping out of trouble for very long!"

CHAPTER EIGHT

"I hate baby sitting," said Molly. She and Lucy sat on the stone wall separating the daisy field from the permanent borders of the afterlife with Lucy. The day was warm and sunny with little puffs of clouds here and there against the blue of the sky. They watched Willie pick daisies and pull their petals off.

Lucy sighed. "I know what you mean, but it was the only way we could get him to deal with the realities of his life." She shook her head. "He's a stubborn one."

Molly chuckled. "He sure was funny the night we reduced him. He was so angry with us. Shouting and cursing at us one minute and reduced to a childish temper tantrum the next, with no memory of how to express it. He must have been a bear to live with."

Lucy sighed again. "Yes, I'd forgotten that such words existed. It was a good thing we reduced him as quickly as we did, or we'd have had to purify the air and ourselves."

They sat in silence for some minutes watching Willie pick flowers, his portly adult body and his childish activities contrasting sharply.

"Not a pretty sight," said Molly. She wrinkled her nose in distaste.

"No." Lucy sighed again. "But it's the only thing we could do."

"Have you ever seen anyone reduced before?" asked Molly.

"Once," said Lucy. "That was a sad case, too. Similar to this one."

"That reducing business is amazing, isn't it?"

"Yes, it's quite a procedure. One minute they're adults in an adult's body, and the next they're children in an adult's body, and they've temporarily forgotten everything that's happened to them beyond the age they've become."

"Who invented that?"

"The spirit of Albert Einstein gave us the principles necessary to create the procedure. He was working with time and space in the physical. The first few instruments they produced weren't very good and they were dangerous to use. It's much safer now."

"Dangerous?" Molly had taken the whole business as an enormous lark, a good joke on Willie.

"Yes, the first ones spread the rays so widely that one or two of the first operators got caught up in them too. By the time anyone found them, they'd wreaked terrible infantile havoc on the procedure room and on the instrument itself. They had taken the whole thing apart, and lost pieces of it. We never did find those. They had a terrible time trying to put the thing back together since the ones that had put it together in the first place had been reduced." Lucy was silent for a few moments watching Willie inspecting stones from the edge of the path from the river.

"So what happened?" Molly's prompt and bright gaze called Lucy back from her reverie.

"Well, they eventually figured out how to rebuild it from the notes the operators had made, and used it to bring the operators back. Since then they've developed protective suits and lined rooms to do the procedure in, and there haven't been any more accidents."

"Problems are real easy to solve here, aren't they?" said Molly.

Lucy laughed a soft little laugh. "Mechanical problems are easy to solve here. We have all the expertise necessary for anything like that. It's the relational and spiritual problems that are difficult."

"Just like in the physical."

Willie ran up to them shouting. "Mommy! Mommy! Look what I brung you!" He handed Lucy a bedraggled bouquet of daisy centres.

"That's just lovely, darling," said Lucy, who had been elected by common consent to act as Willie's mother for the duration of the reduction. She put her arm around his fat body and hugged him. Willie nestled closer and looked up adoringly at Lucy.

"I sure do love you Mommy," he said.

"I love you too, dear," said Lucy. Willie turned and scurried off in search of other treasures in the daisy field.

"Yuck!" said Molly. "How can you stand it?"

"Stand what?" asked Lucy.

"Stand to let him touch you like that?"

Lucy sighed. "It's difficult, but I try to think of him as the child he really is right now, and it doesn't seem so bad. At least he doesn't smell anymore."

Molly laughed at the memory. "Yeah, that was quite a trick trying to get him clean though."

"He's not really clean yet either, and I don't know why, I had the spray on high and I scrubbed him hard. It usually doesn't take more than one easy shower to clean a spirit from the earth plane." Lucy inspected the bouquet that Willie had picked for her. "I'm not sure I have the strength to take him through the personal laundry again. Maybe this little tour of baby land will soften him up a bit."

Suddenly Willie shrieked and ran down the hill, scattering his latest bouquet behind him. Molly and Lucy zoomed rapidly after him. There was a loud splash as Willie upended himself in the brook at the bottom of the hill. He set up a lusty howl when he discovered he was all wet again. "Mommy! Mommy!" he screamed. Tears ran down his whiskered cheeks.

"C'mon Molly, help me hoist him out of here." Lucy grabbed one of Willie's grimy paws. Molly grabbed the other hand with a look of distaste, and together the two spirits tugged Willie to a sitting position. Willie suddenly discovered the joys of the bathtub and began splashing vigorously, thoroughly soaking Molly and Lucy in the process.

"Willie make big splash," he shouted, happily engrossed in his new game.

"Willie sure does," replied Lucy. She sat down on a rock with her back to the sun to dry out. "I wish I'd thought of this before. If I'd known how easy it was to give him a bath I'd have had him down here with a bar of soap instead of trying to take him through that shower at the laundromat."

"He's even getting a little cleaner." Molly stretched out on the ground beside Lucy. "I sure hope this childhood phase doesn't take too long, I'm soaked."

"I hope not either, but it has to last long enough to give him the sense of having been appropriately mothered. He completely missed that experience after the age of five in the physical."

"But his mother was there, wasn't she?" asked Molly.

"She was there, but she abandoned Willie emotionally at that time, so he's been suffering the deprivation ever since. She was a very cold, hard mother. She really shouldn't have been a mother at all."

"Why not?"

"Because she never learned appropriate mothering skills from her mother. She just didn't know how to be loving and supportive. All of her children suffered to some degree or other, but Willie suffered the worst because he was the oldest."

"Humph!" said Molly, "it's a good thing he never had any children. If they were in any worse shape than he's in, the world couldn't stand it!"

"He was aware enough of the shortcomings in himself, and his family, to realize that he would never make a good father. He hated being a child and always vowed he'd never bring a child into the world to suffer as he had."

"Well," said Molly, "it's probably the best decision he's ever made. Shame he couldn't have carried it to other areas of his life." She rolled over to allow her back to dry.

Lucy shrugged and sighed. "Well, that was only a momentary aberration. He's never exhibited such insight since."

Molly glanced over at Willie. "We'd better get him out of there, he's starting to shrivel."

The two spirits jumped to their feet. "C'mon Willie, let's go now. We can come back tomorrow and play for awhile," said Lucy.

"Oh, goody," said Willie, "I like to play in the water." He scrambled to his feet and held out his hand to Lucy. "I'm hungry, Mommy," he said. "Can I have a jam sandwich?"

"What's the magic word?" Lucy took the less grimy paw.

"Please," said Willie. He skipped up the hill beside Lucy.

At Jim's request everyone gathered at the Poste residence the following evening. "Connie called me today," he said as he met them in the yard. As usual the house was ablaze with light. "I guess the problem has increased since the other evening. She's quite terrified." He led the way around the house to Connie's temporary quarters in the greenhouse. They found her huddled on the lounge.

"Connie, tell the others what you've just told me," said Jim after greetings were exchanged.

Connie, looking like a little ghost herself, began her brief story. "It's just the usual, except more of it. There're more things broken than before, and the noise seems to have invaded the whole house equally. I can't even go into the kitchen now." She stifled a sob. "I'm so hungry!"

"How long has it been since you've eaten?" asked Gertrude in some concern.

"Why didn't you just go to a restaurant in town?" asked Mary Ann. "Or call me, I could at least have brought you a sandwich." She sat down beside Connie and put her arms around her.

Tears trickled down Connie's cheeks in spite of herself. "I-I haven't eaten since y-yesterday morning, and then I only had toast." She hugged her blanket closer to herself. "I was making coffee and thanking God that the kitchen was still safe, when all of a sudden it wasn't. It was like a cold wind came through and then the racket began there too." The tears became a flood. She buried her face in her hands and began to sob. "I-I couldn't get to the car because I'd have to go through the back way and that's where the noise was the worst. Besides, I-I d-didn't have the keys. W-willie put them someplace and I-I can't find them."

Don looked at Gertrude and they both shook their heads in disbelief. "But how have you been getting to the hospital?" asked Gertrude.

Connie looked at Gertrude blankly for a moment as if she'd forgotten that she was even there. "I c-called a taxi and I only went once."

"And you said before that the noise was only sometimes in the kitchen," said Mary Ann.

"It came into the kitchen once, at the very beginning, and it hasn't been there since." Connie sniffed and rubbed at her wet nose with the heel of her hand.

"How has the rest of the house been?" asked Jim.

"N-noisy," said Connie. She hiccoughed like a small child. "I-I'm so hungry!"

"I'll go in and get you something to eat in a minute," said Jim. "I want to set the girls to work first." He turned to Mary Ann and Gertrude. "I want you two to go through the house and sense every room. See if you can identify any discarnate personality anywhere in the house. You know the routine, Mary Ann. You can guide Gertrude, since this is her first ghost hunt." He got up and headed for the kitchen. Mary Ann and Gertrude followed him.

"Where should we start?" asked Mary Ann. She filled the kettle and set it on the stove to heat.

Jim rummaged in the cupboard looking for food for

Connie. "I think you'd better start downstairs first, there seems to be less contamination down here and you might pick up some individual vibes more easily with less psychic racket. Pay special attention to the studio though, as that seems to be where the noise is originating." He pulled out a can of vegetable soup, and began to search for a pot to heat it in. "You two look after each other," he said, "that ghost seems to be able to throw things."

Mary Ann and Gertrude began their survey in the library. "I wonder if we should both go into trance at the same time," said Mary Ann. "Jim seemed a little concerned for our safety."

"Why don't I get Don to come with us. He can look after us, and then we can both go into trance. Connie doesn't need two men to look after her." Gertrude headed back out to the greenhouse with Mary Ann close behind.

"C'mon, Don, we need your help." She stopped abruptly. Mary Ann crashed into her from behind.

"Sorry," Mary Ann apologized and looked a little embarrassed.

"You mean you were afraid to stay there even for a minute by yourself?" Gertrude arched an eyebrow at Mary Ann.

"You betcha," said Mary Ann. "I felt unpleasant things in that room, and I wasn't even in trance yet. I wasn't hanging around to let the ghosties get me. If they're coming for me they're going to have to take you too."

"I don't think I want you doing this," said Don.

"Oh, c'mon, Don," said Mary Ann, "nothing's going to happen to Gertrude. Besides we need you to keep the physical safe for us while we're in trance. You know, catch flying ashtrays and things like that." She chuckled again, a gleam of mischief in her bright eyes.

Don sighed and followed them back to the library. I think I'm sorry I said she could do this, he thought. Not that I could have stopped her, or would have wanted to either, he corrected himself. I just wish she'd chosen a safer second career. He took up a stance just inside the library door with his back to the wall so that he could see the whole room at one glance.

Gertrude and Mary Ann quieted themselves on the sofa, and prepared their minds for trance. In a few moments they were searching the atmosphere for negative influences. They saw the subtle changes the room had undergone over the years: wallpaper in one era, paint in others and various draperies on the windows, sometimes matching and sometimes not. The room was still, as if waiting for them to complete their survey and move on. After a thorough search of the room they left the trance state.

"Did you find anything?" asked Mary Ann, when she had opened her eyes again.

"It's the strangest thing," said Gertrude. "For all the noise in this room, there's nothing here. Even Molly wasn't sitting on the mantle shelf, and I really did expect to see her."

"I wonder if we should call her. I've never tried calling a spirit before. They've always just been there whether I wanted them or not."

Gertrude stood up and stretched. "I tried calling her the other day but she didn't respond. She told me a long time ago that if I ever needed her, all I had to do was call her, but it doesn't seem to work quite that way. I'll try again when we go upstairs."

They searched every room on the two main floors of the house with little result. For once the master bedroom was quiet. They began their climb to the attic studio.

"This is really the psychic hot spot of this house," said

Mary Ann. "I can feel whatever it is pushing against me. Whatever's haunting this place doesn't want us around." They continued their climb to the landing, with Don following behind them.

"Now don't you girls be doing anything dangerous. I don't like this excursion one bit."

"Now, Don," said Gertrude. She gave him a brief hug. "You know that Jim said that there was no physical danger from ghosts. If I thought there was, I wouldn't be here." A crash resounded from the room above and they both jumped. "You see, I'm as nervous as you are." She hugged him again. "I think it's quite brave of you to be here at all since you're not a sensitive and have no way of dealing with hidden things like Mary Ann and I do."

Don grunted. "Yes, well, I'm not here because I'm particularly brave. I just don't want anything to happen to you. And if I can help it at all, I'm not going to let it. Now, go and get this over with so we can return to the land of reality again."

All three of them trudged up the stairs and Mary Ann cautiously opened the studio door. The lights burned brightly. "I wonder how much longer these lights are going to last?" Mary Ann visually surveyed the room. "They've been on continuously for almost a week now."

"I think fluorescent lights last for a long time." Don took up a protective position behind Gertrude. "I'm going to stand here and keep an eye on things while you two get on with your work."

Gertrude and Mary Ann positioned themselves in the middle of the room, back to back for protection. "I'm going to call Molly this time and see if she answers," said Gertrude. They settled themselves more comfortably on the floor and began to prepare themselves for trance once more.

Slowly the atmosphere of the room became visible to them. "Chaos, nothing but chaos," muttered Mary Ann, staring off into the ether.

"Lyman's here," said Gertrude, observing her side of the room. "I wonder if he'll talk to me?" She concentrated on the image of Lyman in her mind. "Lyman, Lyman, can you hear me?" she called through the psychic noise.

Lyman lifted his head and looked about him dully.

"Over here, Lyman. I want to talk to you," called Gertrude in her mind.

Lyman's shaggy head swung around toward Gertrude,

the rope he'd used to hang himself still dangling from his neck.

"Are you the one who's haunting this house, Lyman?"

Lyman looked frightened. "Bad man! Bad man!" he said, and faded away.

"Darn!" said Gertrude softly. "Bad man doesn't exactly do it for me, Lyman." She concentrated on Molly and called out to her, hoping for an answer. The wait seemed interminable. She was just about to call again when Molly appeared.

"What DO you want!" she demanded. "I'm busy!" Her caftan was wrinkled and her turban was askew. Wisps of hair escaped around the edges of it. One of her earrings was missing. She floated mid-air, a wilted daisy chain wrapped around her neck.

"Nice to see you too," said Gertrude. "I need some help."

"Well," said Molly belligerently, "I'm waiting."

"Do you know anything about the haunting of this house?"

"Didn't Lyman tell you? You were just talking to him."

"He just said 'bad man.'"

"Well, he's probably telling the truth, he doesn't know

enough to lie."

"Molly, do you know who's haunting this house?"

"I told you already weeks ago that I don't. I don't know any more now either but if it's not Lyman it has to be someone else from the house's past. I've been very busy these past few earth weeks, trying to rehabilitate Willie, who's got the manners and the face of a pig, only not so cute. I've got to go. I left Lucy riding herd on him by herself. See you later." She disappeared.

"Oh, Molly!" said Gertrude. She came out of trance.

"You were talking to Molly?" asked Don.

"Momentarily," said Gertrude. "She was no help."

Mary Ann joined them. "I heard you calling Lyman. Was he there?"

"Briefly. All I got out of him was 'bad man, bad man.'"

"Well that's better than the chaos we had been getting." They were silent for a moment then looked at each other and said in unison. "I wonder if Molly's Willie and our Willie are one and the same?" They laughed at the coincidence.

"Is is even possible? After all, he's not dead yet," said Mary Ann.

Gertrude shrugged. "I wonder how we could find out, Molly's not very available just now."

"I'll check the encyclopedia of all things psychic when I go home," said Mary Ann.

"If you two are finished here, let's get out and discuss this someplace else," said Don. "I've had enough of haunted houses for one evening." He ushered the girls out of the room and closed the door behind them.

"I think I'd like to get another look at that master bedroom," said Mary Ann. "I still can't make head nor tail of why the bathroom should be so neat and the bedroom be such a mess."

"Let's have another look," said Gertrude, "that's been bothering me too. It may just be because of what Marie Perry told us. I wonder if Connie can shed any light on it." They opened the bedroom door and went in.

"I think it's messier than ever," said Mary Ann as she glanced over the room. "I'm going to take a look in the bathroom to see if it's still just as neat." She opened the bathroom door. "It's still spotless. I'm going to see if I can pick up anything in trance this time." She sat down on the edge of the unmade bed and quieted her mind. Suddenly a force of great strength began pushing her over backward onto the bed. Don and Gertrude watched in amazement as they saw Mary Ann lie back against the pillows, a look of pure terror on her face. She could not seem to right herself and appeared to be wrestling with something, so violent were her struggles.

"I wonder if I should try to wake her?" said Gertrude. "It's not good to come out of trance too quickly."

Just then Mary Ann cried out and rolled herself off the bed. The wrinkled green sheets and thick duvet went with her but did not soften the landing. The shock of her body hitting the floor roused her abruptly. She was on her feet in an instant, kicking at the entangling sheets, still dazed from her trance.

"What happened?" asked Gertrude. She went to Mary Ann.

"Don't sit on that bed," said Mary Ann. "Bad things have happened there."

"What kind of bad things?"

Mary Ann shuddered. "I can't describe what I saw." She sat down on a chair. "This room is full of hidden things."

"Why did you lie down?" asked Don moving to the

other side of Mary Ann.

Mary Ann was silent for a moment considering whether she should tell them what happened. He's liable to forbid Gertrude to come with us if I tell what really happened, she thought. She sighed. I have to.

"Well?" asked Don.

"Well," said Mary Ann, "I was pushed."

"Pushed!" said Gertrude. "By what?"

"Not what, whom."

"That's it, that's just it." Don began pacing the room. "Gertrude, I don't want you to be involved in these ghost hunts anymore. They're too dangerous. C'mon, let's get out of here." He started toward the door.

"Oh, Don, just a minute, we can't leave Mary Ann here by herself and she's not ready to move yet," said Gertrude.

"I'm all right," said Mary Ann. "Actually, I'd like to get out of here myself. That experience was enough to give even me the willies." With Gertrude's help she got to her feet, and together they all made their way downstairs.

"So what did you discover?" asked Jim as they entered the greenhouse from the kitchen.

"Not much," said Gertrude, "although we did talk to

Lyman and Molly briefly, and Mary Ann just had a rather harrowing experience in the master bedroom."

Jim looked alarmed. "What happened? I thought you looked kind of pale."

Mary Ann sat down in a patio chair with a thump. "It felt like someone was trying to force his attentions on me while I was in trance."

"His?" asked Jim. "Why his?"

"Because of the strength and the smell. He smelled as if he hadn't washed in several days."

"Phew!" Gertrude laughed. "That in itself would be pretty overwhelming!"

"Not funny!" said Mary Ann, for once not seeing the humour in the conversation. "By the way," she said, turning to Connie, "is there some reason why your bedroom is a dreadful mess while your bathroom is as scrubbed and neat as a pin?"

Connie looked unhappy. "I tidied it the last time I was up there last week. I haven't been up there since." She began playing with her braid.

"Connie," said Gertrude gently, "is there something you're not telling us?"

Connie squirmed. "I don't think so," she said. "I've told you everything I can."

"This is not some giant set-up, is it?" asked Jim.

Connie's eyes widened in alarm. "Oh, no. Of course it isn't," said Connie. "I would never do that, and I really have told you everything I can."

"I hope so," said Jim. "These people are my friends and I don't want them to get hurt."

Gertrude tried another approach. "What was Willie like before his accident?"

"He was a fine artist, and he was known internationally, you can ask anyone." Connie closed her lips firmly.

Gertrude sighed. "Did he have any brothers and sisters?"

"There were six of them, five boys and one girl."

"D'you know where they're living?"

"He's got one brother here in town, but he never sees him. He was at our wedding and I haven't seen him since. I don't think I'd recognize him if I saw him again. I don't know where the rest are, he never talked about them."

"Do you remember his name?"

Connie thought for a minute. "I think it's Peter, but I don't really remember."

"Have you been to see Willie today?" asked Jim.

Connie shrugged. "What's the point? He's in a coma." She pulled the blanket more firmly around herself. "Besides, I still haven't been able to find the keys and taxis are expensive."

"Sometimes coma victims respond more rapidly if they hear the voice of a loved one," said Gertrude.

Connie looked down at her thin hands. "How d'you know so much?"

"I'm a nurse," said Gertrude.

"Oh," said Connie. She tugged at the blanket again.

Silence hung heavily in the room for a few minutes. At last Jim said, "I guess that's all we can do here tonight, we might as well go home and get some shut-eye. Tomorrow is another busy day."

Everyone stood up to leave except Connie who pulled the blanket more tightly still and looked even more distressed than she had been.

"Is there anything I can get you before we leave?" asked Gertrude.

Connie shook her head.

"We'll see you tomorrow night then."

They walked together around the house. Just as they reached the front, the light in the studio winked off. "There's the answer to our question about the light," said Don.

CHAPTER NINE

The next day Jim searched the phone directory for Peter Poste. Peter's wife answered the phone and informed Jim that Peter was the principal of Scott Elementary School and that he could find him there. She hung up with not even a good day.

Hm, thought Jim, if Mrs. Peter's like that, I wonder what Peter's like? He made an appointment for that afternoon with the school secretary.

Peter was a portly man of middle age. He was balding slightly, and his grey hair was lank and greasy-looking. The red Mickey Mouse tie he wore was stained with several former meals. I wonder if bulbous noses run in the Poste family? thought Jim. He made himself comfortable in the one armchair that the office provided. His glance as he seated himself took in the metal utility shelf which held a few dog-eared books, two sports trophies and much dust. Except where Peter's elbows habitually rested, the dust lay undisturbed on the surface of the desk that was not covered in papers.

Peter rocked himself in his desk chair and peered at Jim over tented fingers. "Now, Mr. MacDonald, what can I do for you?" he asked.

"Please call me Jim." He handed Peter his business card.

Peter took the card and peered shortsightedly at it. "You're the ghost hunter." He set the card in the dust at the corner of the desk and resumed his tented finger pose. "I just got through reading an article about you in the Guardian. It's very nice to meet you in the flesh."

Jim chuckled. "That article was only based on the truth, the rest of it was pure fantasy. I guess that's another aspect of the freedom of the press."

"So how may I help you?" Peter picked up the card again and peered at it intently.

"I was called to your brother's house a week or so ago. There have been some strange disturbances there, and I and my colleagues are working with Connie to discover its source."

"Who's Connie?" asked Peter in genuine bewilderment.

Jim had difficulty hiding his surprise. "Connie is Willie's wife," he replied.

Peter reddened. "I thought her name was Cathy. I've only ever seen her once. I don't think I'd even recognize her anymore." He leaned back in his chair again.

"You and Willie weren't close?"

"No, Willie and I parted company years ago. I only went to his wedding on a whim. He didn't invite me and I sure didn't feel at home. I left soon after the reception was over." He frowned. "What do you need to know?"

Jim crossed his knees and adjusted his trouser legs. "As I said, there have been strange things happening at his home. His wife is panicked into sleeping in the greenhouse. There seems to be no physical explanation, so she called me to investigate the paranormal."

Peter rocked forward in his chair and placed his hands in careful alignment on the desk. "D'you mean like ghosts?"

"Well, we don't call them ghosts officially. They're spirits, or in this case it seems to be just ethereal disturbances. My colleagues can't seem to identify any particular spirit that could be perpetrating the noise."

"So what do you want from me?" Peter sat back in his chair and began to rock back and forth again. The chair squeaked in rhythm with his rocking.

"We're investigating the history of the house as far back as we can go. It seems to have been the centre of some very unhappy relationships in the past. I need to know what Willie was like before his accident. Connie doesn't or won't say very much about him."

"Hm," said Peter, "I'm not sure I can enlighten you very much on that either. Like I said, I really haven't been close to him these past twenty years. I do know that he was a world-respected artist, though I never could see much in his splashes myself. I guess others could, but I'm no judge anyway."

Jim sighed. "That's what Connie keeps saying. What was he like growing up?"

"Of course I only knew him from the point of view of the younger brother, but he always seemed to be angry. I know he was awfully hard to get along with."

"Did he fight with the younger ones a lot?"

"No, we were never allowed to fight. Mother always made the punishment worse if we fought. As the old saying goes, she ruled the house with a rod of iron. She ruled Father too. No matter what she did, he never said a word." Peter rocked more vigorously. "Maybe he didn't know. He worked a lot." The chair tipped alarmingly onto its back legs. Peter looked surprised and came forward with a thump. He grabbed the edge of the desk to steady himself and continued. "As a result, we were always very soft-spoken. Mother used to brag about how good we were. The truth of the matter was, we didn't dare to be anything else."

"Where did Willie come in the family?"

"He was the oldest. Mother made him responsible for everything we did from the time he started school. If anything went wrong, she said he was the oldest and should have known better. She always made an example of him."

"Wow!" said Jim. "That's heavy duty stuff for a five-year-old."

"Yes, it was," said Peter. "I think that was why he was so angry all the time. He was never allowed to be a child." He was silent for a few minutes remembering the past. "I don't remember him ever playing."

"Didn't he have any friends?"

"I don't think so. He spent most of his time by himself painting. In those days he used to paint pretty pictures, the kind I could understand."

"How did he come to start painting?"

"I'm not sure. I think he got one of those 'teach yourself to paint' kits for Christmas one year, from Aunt Belle. She dabbled a little. She was Mother's sister. She gave each of us something unique to learn the Christmas of our eighth year. She gave me a child's violin. It really worked. I still play violin today."

"So Aunt Belle was kind to you children."

"She was an eminently sensible woman, quite unlike Mother. She was the only one that Willie got along with. I think she actually liked him."

"Was he an unpleasant child?" asked Jim.

Peter took a deep breath, puffed out his cheeks, and held the breath for a moment while he pondered his brother's personality. "I don't think he was that way from choice," he said at last. "None of us were allowed to be children. I think that was the basis of his nastiness. I know he was a very angry young man."

"How did he express his anger?"

Peter shrugged. "Through his painting, I guess. It was the only avenue open to him of a civilized nature."

Jim shook his head in amazement. "I'm not surprised at the things I've been hearing about him then."

Peter sat back in his chair abruptly. "What things?" He scowled at Jim.

"I had occasion to hear that his relationships with women were always difficult."

"I guess a person could say that."

"How did he feel about your mother after all that?"

Peter pursed his lips for a moment. "He hated her," he said at last.

"Do you know that for sure?"

"Yes. He told me that once. He said that she was the cause of all his trouble. That was the only time he ever said anything about our upbringing. He was very close-mouthed that way. He'd never confide in anyone."

"Did he ever have therapy for all his problems?"

"No, he always scorned psychiatrists. He said they'd take away his creativity by analyzing him. He would laugh and say that artists had to suffer."

"Do you think he suffered?"

"I'm quite sure he did, and when the pain got too great, he'd make others suffer too."

"Why do you say that?"

"I've talked with his ex-wife. She told me a lot about their relationship. She's married to Max Perry now. I guess from what she said, Willie really did a job on her psychologically. He'd do something really nasty and then be sorry he did it, and apologize and fall all over himself to be nice to her. He did it once too often and she finally left."

"How'd he take that?"

"I'm not sure. That was after he told me to get lost. I think he shut himself up out there for quite a long time and then all of a sudden there was the announcement of his coming marriage to Cathy."

"Connie," said Jim.

"Sorry," said Peter.

"What did you and Willie fight about that caused such a rift?"

Peter scowled, then sighed. "I don't really want to think about that." He was silent for several minutes, then, his scowl darkened even further. He said, "I was so angry with him I felt like I could just smash his face in, and enjoy it too!" His knuckles whitened as his big hands grasped the arms of his chair. "Even now I have to remind myself that he was only trying to relieve some of his own pain, and I feel I'm being charitable even giving him that much."

"It must have been very devastating for you," said Jim.

Peter rocked in his chair with renewed vigour, his hands still clenching the arms. "Sometimes I can't believe how angry I can get over it even now," he said through clenched teeth. "I'm sorry, I try not to think about it anymore." He relaxed his hands and stretched his fingers. "I rarely ever talk about it. Very few people even know what happened."

"Can you tell me about it?"

Peter rocked forward in his chair. "For Cathy's sake I will."

"Connie," said Jim.

Peter leaned forward on his elbows shielding his face with his hands. "It was when I applied for a principalship the first time. I wasn't married then. I was really excited about it and told him what I was hoping for. I was still pretty young, but I did have a few years experience behind me, and I thought I could get it. It was at a smaller school than this, so I thought I had a good chance. He just laughed at me. He said that he'd heard from some of the parents that the children had complained about me, that I was a useless teacher, and that I'd be lucky to even still be working by that time next year. He was teaching art on an itinerant basis for the school district then, so the remarks had a certain credibility."

"What did you do?" asked Jim.

"Well, needless to say, I felt like killing him." Peter sat back, his meaty hands curled themselves into tight fists on the arms of his chair again. "However, I didn't. I was so disoriented by his attack that I could hardly even defend myself. I just went home and suffered alone for a long time. It's hard to put that kind of thing into perspective when it comes from someone you should be able to trust. No matter how I tried to rationalize what he'd said, the fact that he'd included unnamed others in the assessment made it far worse. I could dismiss his pronouncements as those of a warped mind coming from anger and hatred, but I couldn't dismiss the assessment of the parents and their children." He began to rock vigorously again. "And how do you find out the truth about that kind of remark? You can't very well go to the parents, and which parents would you go to?"

"What happened then?"

"Oh, I tried to be friends with him still. I told myself that the problem was his, not mine. I assessed all my evaluations, which were very good, by the way, but I could never feel the same about what I was doing. Needless to say, I didn't get the job. The interview was terrible, mainly because I was feeling so awful about myself and my abilities. You see, what he'd implied, besides what he'd actually said, was that I was a rotten person too, and that's hard to live with." The rocking continued at a slightly faster pace.

"That would be very hard to cope with," said Jim. "I wonder why it hit you so hard?"

"I think because of my upbringing."

"But yours was the same as his, wasn't it?"

"Yes, it was. And that's just exactly why he could do that to me like that. My insecurities were the same as his and he knew that. His method of making himself feel better about himself was to smash other people with their shortcomings. Mine was to be kind and helpful, which is why I chose to be a teacher. It's curious isn't it, how two people from the same family learn different coping skills."

"It's a wonder you didn't just give up," said Jim. "It must have been very difficult to keep going."

"It was that," said Peter. "And I did give it up for awhile, but I was never happy doing what I was doing. I'd just met Betty, my wife. She's a saint. She was very patient with my insecurities and gave me encouragement. It was still a long time before I could even tell her what had happened. Anyway, after a year or two of roaming aimlessly around, I decided to try again. Actually, I ran into the principal of my old school and I ended up telling him the whole grimy story and he convinced me to return to teaching. He said I had a way with elementary school children and should be teaching. He also said that he'd never heard of any complaints about me from parents, so I guess it was just Willie's warped mind in action."

"Such havoc he created," said Jim. "I wonder if he's done it to others?"

"Oh, I wouldn't be surprised. I know what Marie said about him and their relationship. I expect that Cathy's had the same sort of trouble with him. Maybe even worse since she's younger."

"Connie," said Jim.

"Sorry," said Peter.

"You might want to talk to Marie sometime. I'm sure she could give you lots of insight into the workings of Willie's convoluted mind." The rocking slowed and his fists relaxed into hands again. He rubbed his face, and his scowl eased a little.

"I've already talked to her," said Jim. "My colleagues interviewed Max Perry and he said that she didn't talk about it anymore, and would really prefer not to, but when I phoned her the other day she did agree to talk to me."

"I guess it's a pretty painful memory for her too."

"I can certainly see why."

A bell rang distantly, signalling the end of classes for the day. Jim rose from his chair and held out his hand to Peter. "You've certainly been a great help to us." He shook Peter's hand. "Thanks." He turned to go.

"I only hope you can help Cathy. If she needs anything let me know and I'll do what I can."

"Connie," said Jim.

❖

Jim pulled his chair up to his kitchen table and sat down. "I think we need to assess our situation now," he said. "A review of the available information is in order. We'll start with you and Gertrude, Mary Ann."

"I don't think we know very much." Gertrude frowned.

"Of course we do," said Mary Ann. "We know that the house is disturbed. We know it's not Lyman, so it must have some other source."

"Well, that's not really very much. It's mostly what it isn't, not what it is," said Gertrude.

"True, but we have to eliminate what it isn't before we can say what it is."

"Mary Ann's right." Jim leaned onto one elbow, picked up his pen and prepared to take notes. "I interviewed Willie's brother, Peter, today. He said that Willie had a very difficult upbringing and as a result, all of his relationships were skewed and unhappy. He didn't add a lot to what we already know."

"Certainly relationship difficulties can happen in a situation like that," said Don. "I'd be interested to know what Peter's experience was like, to compare the results."

"I guess his was the same, only he handled it differently,"

said Jim. "I forgot to ask him how his relationships were. I know he's married because I was talking to Mrs. Poste on the phone today. She was kind of rude but Peter claims she's a saint."

"I don't think that matters," said Don. "We're investigating Willie's environment, not Peter's."

"True." Jim smiled. "I guess I'm just nosey."

"It may only show a reflection of the birth order anyway." Don eased the crease in his trousers and crossed his knees. "Along with differences in personality, birth order has a fair influence on how people handle stress and mental and emotional discomfort."

"Could it just be an accumulation of psychic distress over the years that's causing the disturbances at Willie's?" asked Gertrude.

"It could be," said Mary Ann, "but I don't think so, not after my experience in the bedroom there." She shivered at the memory. "I can still smell him."

"I wish Molly was more forthcoming these days," said Gertrude. "She was always underfoot before, especially when I didn't want her there."

"Yes, well, that's Molly for you," said Mary Ann. "She's

probably got some other big project going just now."

"She did say she and Lucy were looking after Willie. She says he has the face and manners of a pig." Gertrude laughed. "She didn't say whether he was in the physical or not. I do wish I could talk to her for at least a few minutes."

"Why don't you try calling her again?" said Jim. "Tell her we really need her input, even if it is just for five minutes."

"I think she's getting impatient with me." Gertrude made a annoyed face. "The last time she just breezed in and breezed out again and was very short-tempered, even for her."

"Let's try anyway," said Mary Ann. "I'll go with you. I haven't seen Molly for a long time and I rather like her. I get a kick out of her gruff directness."

They prepared themselves for trance and slipped into the open concentration of their minds. "Molly, Molly," called Gertrude. There was no immediate response. "Molly, Molly," she called again with more force.

"What is it you want?" asked Molly. "I told you before I'm busy!" She settled herself on the mantle shelf and arranged her purple and gold caftan around her ankles.

"I'm sorry to disturb you," said Gertrude, "but we really do need your help."

"You're not a bit sorry," snapped Molly, "you're just being polite." She hitched her shoulders and straightened her sequined turban to a less rakish angle. It had become dislodged, so fast was her trip to Gertrude's call.

Gertrude sighed. "You're right, Molly, I was just being polite. It's the way I was brought up, and you did tell me that if I ever needed your help all I'd have to do was call and you'd come."

"I did say that, didn't I," said Molly somewhat less peevishly. "Well, get on with it, then, what do you want?"

"We have a haunting that we're having difficulty getting to the bottom of," said Gertrude.

"All we can figure out is that it's a man," said Mary Ann.

"Oh, you're here too, are you?" said Molly. "I didn't notice you before."

"Thanks," said Mary Ann. "I always wondered how memorable I am."

Molly glared at her. "So what makes you think that it's a man?"

"It has the strength of a man and it smells like a man."

"Therefore it must be a man," interrupted Molly. "I told you already, his name's Willie. He sure smells if we don't dunk him every day!"

Gertrude sat up straighter. "What's his last name?"

"Poste, and he's just visiting. Lucy and I have to babysit him while he's here. He's some artist from the physical, and he sure is a handful!"

"That's our Willie," said Mary Ann.

"So he really is on the other side," said Gertrude. "We were wondering whether he could be in two places at once. What did the Psychic Encyclopedia have to say on the subject, Mary Ann?"

"Not a lot. It really wasn't very instructive. I guess it doesn't happen very often."

"Maybe it happens more often now since we have more sophisticated means of keeping people alive. How old is your encyclopedia?"

"About 1920, I think."

"You need to update your library," said Molly. "Get on with it, then. I'm eager to hear the rest of the story." She leaned forward on the mantle shelf nearly losing her balance in her eagerness.

"Yes, that's the haunting we've been investigating. It's at Willie Poste's, and we can't seem to get a handle on who or what's doing it," said Gertrude. "Jim's interviewed everyone we could contact who's had some connection with the house, but so far nothing's shown up that would concretely point to any one person or event."

Mary Ann sat up straighter in her chair. "I wonder if Willie really could be causing this and it's not a haunting at all?"

Molly sat back and shrugged her ethereal shoulders. "Maybe it's just an accumulation of events, or something else altogether."

Just then a piercing cry for help vibrated through the ether. Everyone jumped, even those in the physical, so intense was the cry.

"That was Lucy!' said Molly. "I've got to go." She disappeared immediately from the shelf, a faint breeze the evidence of her swift passage.

"Wow!" said Mary Ann, as they came out of trance simultaneously, "Lucy must be in some kind of trouble for her to shriek like that."

"What's going on over there?" asked Jim in some alarm.

"Lucy's in some kind of trouble," said Gertrude. "How did you know?"

"We heard her scream." Don took a deep breath to calm his jumpy nerves. "It sent shivers down my spine."

The phone began to ring, more stridently than usual it seemed.

"Mine too," said Jim. He went to answer the phone.

It was Connie. She was in her usual state of tears and panic. "It's Willie!" she sobbed. "He's taken a turn for the worse again."

"Do you want us to come over?" Jim asked.

"I don't know." Connie sniffled. "The noise is just awful right now, and they want me to go to the hospital to be with him." Her voice quavered. "I'm s-so s-scared."

"Why don't you do that then? We'll come over and house-sit while you're gone. We may be able to get a better fix on what's actually happening if you're not there. Will you do that?"

"Y-yes, if you think I should." Connie's voice wobbled.

"I do," said Jim. "Now go and get yourself ready, and we'll be right over." He hung up the phone, and turned back to the room.

"Hi ho, hi ho, it's off to work we go. That was Connie. It seems that Willie's taken a turn for the worse."

Molly returned to the daisy field with a thump, nearly running down Lucy who was desperately holding onto Willie's shirt, and trying to calm him down.

"Oh, Molly, I'm so glad you're here again. Help me. I've had such a time with him all evening. He keeps trying to go through the gates." She shifted her grasp on Willie's shirt tail.

Molly grabbed him by the feet and abruptly upset him. "There!" she said with some satisfaction as she sat down on him, "that should hold him for awhile."

Lucy released her hold on his shirt and flexed her fingers. "Phew!" she said in relief, "I didn't have much strength left."

"I'm sorry I left you by yourself for so long," said Molly. She rarely apologized for anything. "I was just coming out of choir rehearsal and Gertrude called. She called rather forcefully, so I thought I'd better go and see what she wanted. I didn't mean to be so long."

Lucy sighed and straightened her skirt. "That's okay," she said. "I was beginning to think that I'd have to let him go, and you know what that means."

"Yeah," said Molly, "we couldn't send him back. It would be a heavenly calamity to be stuck with him for eternity." Willie regained his breath and began to wriggle underneath Molly. "Sit still, you!" She grabbed him by the ear. "Or I'll have to put you in a straight jacket."

Lucy laughed at the spectacle. "Oh, Molly, there are no straight jackets here."

"Well, whatever the heavenly equivalent is," said Molly. "What're we going to do with him? I can't sit on him forever."

"I don't know," said Lucy, "I guess we'll just have to watch him."

"That won't do, and you know it." Molly was silent for a moment while she thought things over. Suddenly her eyes sparkled. "I know what we'll do," she said. "We'll put him on a leash!" She manifested a short red leash and collar.

"I wish Larry would come by," said Lucy. "I'd really like to have him here now. We need his advice. Willie doesn't seem to be improving with age."

"Larry left choir rehearsal early. He didn't say where he was going, not even to Cecilia. She was a little put out with him, I think. Gregory wasn't there today either."

Lucy bent and began fastening the collar on Willie. "So who played for you?"

"Someone I didn't know," said Molly. She rolled off Willie. "Some kid I hadn't seen before. He was blond and had a wonderful tan, and could he ever play."

"I think that must have been Harry. He just came over a few weeks ago. He was a virtuoso in the physical. His plane crashed on a flight over the Rockies."

Willie got to his feet with a grunt, and took off toward the gate again, but the leash and collar forcefully applied by Molly stopped him in his tracks. He toppled to the ground and lay there panting and sweating.

"I wish Larry would come," said Lucy again. "He seems to be avoiding us lately. Ever since Willie came over, his visits have been getting shorter and shorter, and he's had less and less to say."

"Humph!" said Molly. "I say we don't need him. We're doing just fine on our own. Where's Willie now in his reduction?"

"He's a pre-teen just now, and becoming very hard to handle, and how can you say we don't need Larry?" asked Lucy. "You don't know what you're doing, and I barely know what I'm doing, what if we do the wrong thing?"

"Look, if Larry won't help us, we'll just have to do it on our own. Besides, if doing the wrong thing means that we're stuck with Wee Willie here in his present condition, I'm not going to make any mistakes if I can help it."

Willie rolled to his knees, and Molly gave a gentle tug on the leash. "Down boy!" Willie sat back on his fat haunches and looked at Molly with respect dawning in his piggy eyes.

"I'll be good," he said.

CHAPTER TEN

Willie was having a difficult time in the physical as well.

His heart stopped beating and his blood pressure dropped several times that night. Each time he was resuscitated. Between resuscitations Connie sat by his bedside not touching him, her head bowed as if in prayer.

"Poor little Mrs. Poste," said one of the nurses to the other, "this must be very hard for her. You can see she really cares for him."

"She's very young to have to go through all this," said her colleague. "I wonder what she'll do if he dies. It'll be a pure miracle if he makes it."

The first nurse shrugged. "Cope, I suppose. That's all she can do." They went back to their charting.

Connie couldn't bear to touch Willie. She sat in the worn vinyl chair beside the bed staring out the corner of her eye at Willie's greasy body. I don't know how nurses can stand to touch sick people, she thought, they're always so sweaty and unpleasant.

Gradually her mind wandered to the idea of life after Willie. She smiled a tiny smile in the corners of her mouth. I'll be able to study art again, she thought. That would be sheer heaven! She suddenly realized the enormity of what she was thinking. Her smile faded abruptly. I hope he doesn't die, she thought. She looked over her shoulder to see if anyone had heard her thought. The nurses at the desk continued with their work. Connie relaxed a little.

Willie's machines wheezed and gurgled and occasionally beeped. The lines on the screen above Willie's bed made a regular pattern, green against black, except when they didn't, once every few minutes. His IV dripped steadily on, the amounts carefully controlled by the pump at the head of the bed.

The overlying silence was thick and heavy. Connie's head drooped and she pulled herself up with a jerk. She stretched in the too-large chair and changed her position a little. Her back ached. Again her thoughts wandered. I wonder what he'll be like if he survives, she thought. She recalled all the horror stories she'd heard of the results of brain damage to people's personalities. I wonder if he'll change much, she thought. She imagined life with a post-traumatic Willie. The thought sent shivers down her spine. Maybe he'll improve. I just hope he's not physically impaired. I don't know if I could handle that.

The night dragged silently onward. Willie seemed to be holding his own.

At Connie's telephone call, Jim picked up his ghost hunting kit, which he always kept packed and ready to go. Betsy whined with anticipation. "Not this time Betsy," said Jim. "Stay!" Betsy settled herself beside the stove again, her brown and white bulk relaxing into the little warmth left from the suppertime fire. She whined once and closed her eyes, feigning sleep.

"Mary Ann, you can ride with me. Connie said she'd leave the greenhouse door open for us." Jim unplugged the coffee maker. "If you can't stay the whole night, Don, I'll see that Gertrude gets home in the morning."

Don looked distressed. "What time do you think you'll be through there? I can come and get her."

"Sunrise should see us finished," said Jim.

They arrived at the Poste residence, which, as usual, was far from silent. "It doesn't seem to matter whether Connie is here or not," said Gertrude, as they congregated on the lawn.

"It seems to be a very angry ghost," said Mary Ann. "We know it can't be Willie as he's not dead yet but maybe we could ease some of its pain, whoever it is."

"Ease his pain?" said Don. "That's a pretty tall order. I can't even do that for some of my physical patients. I don't see how you expect to do it for a non-physical one."

Mary Ann shrugged. "It's what we have to do, though. The only way we can stop a haunting is to ease the psychic burden on whoever's doing the haunting."

"Our biggest problem here seems to be discovering the source for sure," said Jim. He started off around the house with the others close behind. "Good, she remembered to leave the door open for us."

They settled themselves in the greenhouse to hear Jim's instructions for the evening. "I'm going to try a technique

I read about last year," he said, as he began pulling tape recorders out of his duffel bag. "It's been around since the advent of the tape recorder but only in the last few years has there been some research into recording the voices of the dead on tape. I'm not convinced of the validity of it, but we're not getting anything any other way, and since Connie isn't here tonight I'd like to try and see what we'll get. We'll at least know for sure if she has any influence on what's happening here." He lined up the tape recorders on the table and began changing the batteries. "I figure with new tapes and new batteries, if there's anything there that can show up on tape, it will."

"What do you want us to do?" asked Gertrude. She began pulling the cellophane off the tapes.

"I want you and Mary Ann to spend at least an hour in each room, psychically listening for anything you can hear. I figure if there's anything to be heard, given enough time you two should be able to hear it."

"What's enough time?" asked Don. Sarcasm was not his usual behaviour and it didn't sit well on him.

Jim looked at him and frowned. "Look, I know you worry about Gertrude, but I've told you before there's nothing going to hurt her." He stacked the tape recorders on top of each other. "Now this is her job, if you don't want her to do it, that's between the two of you, but if she's going to do it, she'll have to do it with full concentration, and you've got to leave her alone and let her do it. She's no use to me if she's trying to placate you all the time. It takes too much of her energy, and she's too valuable a psychic to have her energy drained like that."

"Maybe I should just go home," snapped Don. "I can at least go to sleep and shut it all out."

"Maybe you should." Jim turned away. "Are you girls ready to try listening?" He picked up the stack of tape recorders and started into the house with them.

Gertrude stayed behind for a moment to have a word with her husband. "Don, what's gotten into you, fighting with Jim like that? You know we agreed that I would come to work for him."

Don looked miserable. "I know," he said, "but I get so scared for you, it's making me irritable. Maybe I really should go home and just come back in the morning."

"Maybe you should." Gertrude gave him a hug. "It will certainly make my work a lot easier." She gave Don a little push in the direction of the door. "Now go. I'll see you in the morning."

Gertrude caught up with Jim and Mary Ann as they were setting up the tape in the master bedroom. "D'you really expect to record anything on these?" She cleared a place on the dressing table for the tape recorder.

"I don't really know what I expect," replied Jim. "We've tried about everything else, now it's time to get goofy."

"The people who invented this technique probably don't think it's so goofy," said Mary Ann. She switched on the machine, picked up the remaining tapes and headed for the attic stairs.

"No," agreed Jim, "but I've never used it. It'll be just a wild try on my part. I won't even know how to evaluate it if we do actually get anything on the tapes. I just hope you two hear something tonight."

"Why should we hear anything more tonight, than we did any other night?" asked Gertrude. They made their way up to the studio.

"I think Connie may be having an effect on the atmosphere of this house," said Jim. "She's still young enough to generate some poltergeist activity, and she's certainly troubled enough."

"I wish we knew what she was hiding," said Mary Ann. "It must be something really dreadful for her to behave so secretively with us when she's asked us to help her."

"People have the funniest ideas of what's shameful and should be hidden," said Gertrude. "Don says that everyone thinks that their secrets are the absolute worst, and when you actually find out what they are, they're no worse than anyone else's."

"So it's mostly in our heads, is it?" Mary Ann opened the studio door. The musty smell of unwashed flesh greeted them.

"Phew!" said Jim. "Whoever was in here last couldn't have bathed for about a week"

"That's unusual," said Mary Ann. "It didn't smell like this when we were here before."

"No, it didn't." Gertrude wrinkled her nose in distaste. "I don't care for the aftershave either." A pile of books on the shelf toppled over. Everyone jumped.

"Somebody didn't like your comments about their aftershave," said Jim, as he set up the tape recorder and tested it. "Let's get out of here now for awhile and let these little machines do their work. You two can start work in the library." They trudged back downstairs. "D'you think you can maintain a trance state for an hour at a time, Gertrude?"

"I think so. If I'm just listening it shouldn't be too hard, although it may get monotonous and my attention may slip. At any rate, I'll try." She and Mary Ann turned in at the library door.

"Call us in an hour so we won't have to think about keeping time," said Mary Ann.

"What do you want us to do with the tapes while we're listening?" asked Mary Ann.

"Just let them run, and we'll see what we get." Jim retired to the kitchen to make himself a cup of coffee.

"Where're we going to sit?" Gertrude surveyed the room.

"Someplace comfortable," said Mary Ann. "I'm going to put my feet up if I can." She settled herself in a wing chair with a footstool in front of it.

"I guess I'm for the sofa, then," said Gertrude. "It's cold in here."

"It's the ghosties." Mary Ann chuckled. "They've come to see what we're doing." She snuggled deeper into the chair and closed her eyes. "I hope I don't just fall asleep," she mumbled as her mind drifted off into trance.

I hope not either, thought Gertrude as she surveyed her friend across the room. I don't want to be the only one hearing things. She made herself comfortable on the sofa and began her trance-inducing routine. In a few moments she was seeing the room across the years. The psychic noise was deafening. Doesn't anyone do anything in this room besides fight? she wondered.

An old man and an old woman in the dress of a century ago were hard at it in front of the fireplace. Gertrude couldn't make out all their words, but she saw the old man raise his hand and strike out at the old woman. She hit him back with such force that he upended in the wood box where he stuck, shrieking and yelling curses and obscenities at her, his legs kicking wildly and futilely in the air in an effort to free himself. Slowly the sound of weeping penetrated the scene and overlaid itself on the noise of the argument. The room became shadowy and Gertrude could make out nothing in the room. The weeping continued for some time, sad and helpless and hopeless. Across the room in the physical, Mary Ann snored gently in the wing chair.

In Gertrude's mind the weeping gave way to merriment

and laughter and the sound of breaking glass. Some party, she thought. I wonder who's here? She looked around and observed a variety of people, both children and adults, eating and drinking and dancing. Their clothing reflected the taste and styles of the forties. Gertrude caught the name of 'Gus,' to which a small rosy child responded, and the scene faded.

Scenes piled themselves on top of scenes over the course of the hour, with no regard for time or order. Sometimes they were superimposed on each other, a jumble of noise and events. At other times they were single scenes darkened by time. The underlying tone of the room was one of disorder and basic unhappiness. Gertrude felt weighted down by it all and longed for the hour to be over.

Jim wakened her by gently stroking her hands. She sighed and sat up. "Such confusion," she said.

Mary Ann snored softly on in her chair. Jim shook her gently by the shoulders. "Sleeping on the job again," he said when she had awakened.

"I guess so." She chuckled. "I knew I shouldn't have gotten so comfortable." She stood up, yawned and stretched. "What did you see?" she asked Gertrude.

"Let's get out of here and talk about this someplace else," said Gertrude. "I'm exhausted!"

"A cup of coffee will fix that," said Jim. "I just made a pot." He led the way to the kitchen. "I made us some sandwiches too. I thought you might be hungry after your labours." They seated themselves around the kitchen table. "So what did you see?" Jim passed the refreshments.

"Lots." Gertrude helped herself to two sandwiches from a flowered plate. "That room has experienced more fights and unhappiness than I've known in about twelve lifetimes."

"Did you get a fix on anyone?" Mary Ann pulled her chair in and took a sandwich.

"Sort of," replied Gertrude. She related her observations to the other two. "In one of the more recent scenes there was a little girl called Gus."

"I wonder if that would be the Gus that I visited with?" said Jim. "Her aura is certainly strong enough now to have left an imprint on the ether if it was that strong when she was a child."

Gertrude finished her sandwiches and licked her fingers for want of a napkin. "Well, I'm ready to try another room," she said.

"Let's go." Mary Ann started out to the hall. "I believe the master bedroom's next."

"Aren't you afraid after what happened there the last time?" asked Gertrude. She followed Mary Ann closely up the stairs.

"Yes, but I might as well do this with enthusiasm and energy. I have to do it anyway and it's easier to do it in a positive frame of mind than in a negative one." She started up the stairs to the second floor. "Besides, if I do this positively, it gives me some protection from negative influences. You'll be there too this time, don't forget."

Gertrude sighed. "I know. I just hope you don't fall asleep this time and leave me all alone in there."

"I won't. Not in that room," said Mary Ann. "And you can bet your boots that I won't sit down on the bed either." She opened the door to the room cautiously, then seeing that it was in its usual disturbed state she announced their arrival into the tape recorder.

Again they settled themselves for trance. As they drifted into concentration the room darkened somewhat. The sound of sobbing broke through the ether. A large, shadowy form leaned over a small huddled form on the bed. The long thick braid on the smaller one was unmistakeable. A mist of terror invaded the room. The musty smell was overwhelming. The scene shifted to an earlier time.

A woman lay on the bed straining in the agony of childbirth. The old midwife assisting her hovered in the shadows. "It won't be long now," drifted into Gertrude's mind.

Another contraction gripped the woman. The midwife positioned herself beside the bed. "Push!" echoed across time. The woman pushed, and pushed again. At last the midwife held up the slimy infant by its heels. "It's dead," she said with satisfaction in her voice as the scene faded.

Sobbing intruded itself in Gertrude's mind again, and the huddled figure on the bed reappeared. She was curled into a foetal position, her hair, no longer braided, her only covering. Presently the crying subsided into childlike sniffles, and she rose from the bed. Donning a robe of uncertain colour, she moved to the bedroom door and tried to open it. It was firmly locked. "Bastard!" she screamed, and beat her fists in helpless frustration against the panels.

Gertrude found herself slipping out of trance just as Jim

came to waken them. She was breathing hard and perspiring with the force of the emotion generated by the scene she had just experienced. She opened her eyes and looked around dazedly. "Oh, you're here already," she said to Jim. "Is Mary Ann back yet?"

A small moan from Mary Ann's corner indicated her imminent return to the physical. Her facial expression showed the distress of the scenes she had also witnessed. She wakened to immediate alertness. "Did you see what I saw?" she asked Gertrude.

"I think so," Gertrude nodded. "Connie?"

"Yeah." Mary Ann stood up and stretched. "Let's get out of here, I can't stand this room any longer right now." She headed toward the door. It wouldn't open. "It's stuck," she said as she rattled the knob.

"Here, let me try," said Jim. He grabbed the knob and tugged at the door. It didn't budge. He tugged harder. It still didn't move.

"Why'd you close it?" asked Gertrude of Jim.

"I didn't," he replied. "It must have swung shut after I came in. I didn't really notice." He pulled at the knob again. "There's no cause to panic, I'll get it open."

"Not without a key, you won't," said Gertrude looking more closely at the knob assembly. "The bolt's in place."

"You've got to be kidding!" exclaimed Jim and Mary Ann in unison, as ghostly laughter echoed into the physical.

They looked at one another. "What're we going to do now?" asked Mary Ann.

"I sure don't want to stay in here, not with giggling ghosts at least," said Gertrude.

"The ghosts won't hurt you," said Jim. "If I can find something to jimmy that lock, I'll have us out in a minute." He began searching the room. "Mary Ann, you look in the bathroom; Gertrude, you can look through that dresser. I need something to use as a pry."

A search of the room turned up a ball point pen, a nail file, two hairpins, and a child's magnet.

"This is a very poorly equipped bedroom," said Jim. He tried each item in turn. The pen fit so tightly he couldn't move it after he had inserted it into the crack between the door and the jamb, the nail file broke, the hairpins bent, and the magnet slipped out of his grasp, fell with a little clatter and slid out of reach beneath the door. "Damn!" said Jim, "I almost had it too." Again the room was filled with ghostly laughter.

"I guess all we can do now is wait for Don to come in the morning," said Gertrude.

"But I was supposed to drive you home."

"Oh, yes," said Gertrude. "I'd forgotten that." She sighed.

"So we're here until Connie returns," said Mary Ann, sitting down in her armchair. "I don't mind too much, I can get some sleep. I just wish it wasn't this particular room."

"I'm going to try that door one more time," said Jim reaching for the knob. He tugged mightily and the door opened abruptly sending him staggering backwards to land in Mary Ann's lap with a grunt.

"Get up, you great bear!" gasped Mary Ann. Jim scrambled from his awkward position. They all looked at one another.

"The door's open," giggled Mary Ann. "Last one down's a rotten egg!" They raced for the door and hurried downstairs.

They composed themselves in the greenhouse. "Anyone want coffee?" asked Jim, when he'd caught his breath.

"Only if you'll go in and get it," said Mary Ann. "I've had enough of spirit sports and giggling ghosts for the moment."

Presently they were all seated around the patio table in the lamp-lit greenhouse sipping coffee. It was still several hours until dawn although the moon had already set.

"So what did you two see this time?" asked Jim.

"Connie," said Mary Ann.

"And she was very unhappy," said Gertrude.

"Could you get a fix on her age?" asked Jim.

"No, she looked the same as she always does. Her hair may have been a little shorter," said Mary Ann.

"I sure would've liked to know what had gone on before that scene," said Gertrude. "I wonder if that shadowy figure was Wee Willie."

"It probably was," said Jim, "since she's only been here when he's been here."

"Unless, of course, it was an intruder who'd violated her in some way." Mary Ann stirred two heaping teaspoons of sugar into her coffee and began to stir.

"Is there some way we can get a good look at Willie?" Gertrude sat back and cradled her coffee cup in her hands to keep them warm.

"I don't know if it would do much good," said Mary Ann. "I've only ever seen newspaper photos of him, and

I'm not sure I'd recognize him from those. They weren't very good."

"There're photos in the living room on the piano," said Jim. "I don't know who they are, I didn't look that closely at them when I was in there. Maybe there's one of the two of them together and we could see what he looks like in more detail."

"Will you go get them?" said Mary Ann. "I don't feel like contending with ghosts right now."

"Chicken!" Jim rose to retrieve the photos from the living room.

"It's very wearing being a sensitive," said Mary Ann. "You wouldn't know about that though, not being one."

In a minute Jim was back with the photos. "This looks like a wedding picture," he said. Connie was carrying a bouquet and dressed in pale pink.

"Ugly, isn't he." Gertrude peered at the picture.

"He isn't very pretty," said Mary Ann. "He's certainly fat enough to be the shadowy figure too." She studied the photo for a minute or two. "Oh, I don't know," she said, "it's so hard to tell from a picture."

Gertrude looked closely at the other pictures. "He's not

so much fat as big and lumpy," she observed.

"Yeah," said Mary Ann. "Ugly!" A crash echoed inside the house.

"Watch what you're saying," said Jim, "he's liable to come and haunt you."

"Oh, be quiet, Jim, he can't."

"You don't know that," said Jim. "Maybe that's what's been happening at the hospital this evening. Maybe he's already joined Molly and Lucy permanently on the other side."

"I hope he's not as awful as people say he is or Molly and Lucy have their hands full," said Gertrude.

"His name was Willie and I thought we'd agreed that it was probably our Willie," said Mary Ann.

"You know, I think we may be right. But he's still in the hospital. He'd have to be awfully far gone for them to have him over there."

"The guy's in a coma. How far gone do you have to be before the likes of Molly and Lucy take over?" Jim refilled his mug and offered the pot to the two psychics.

"I don't know," said Gertrude. "They didn't teach us that in nursing school."

Mary Ann giggled. "Spooks and Spirits 101!"

Gertrude groaned. "I can just see old Miss Prince teaching a course like that. She was such a dry old stick."

"Well, it doesn't matter anyway," said Jim, "there's nothing we can do about him if he is over there, so if you two are ready and willing, we'll get back to some spiritual eavesdropping. Maybe we can figure out why he's haunting the house right now and how he's doing it."

"I'm not closing any doors this time," said Mary Ann swallowing the last of her coffee, "once was enough of that foolishness."

"I'm ready." Gertrude pushed back her chair. "I hope we see something tonight. All I got the last time was a lot of noise and that brief communication from Lyman about the bad man."

"Have you got a key to that room, Jim?" asked Mary Ann.

"No, but I'm going to take a screwdriver with me from now on. There's one in the kitchen cupboard."

They trudged up the stairs to the attic again. "That light is still out," said Mary Ann.

"Do you really need it?" asked Jim. "The other one is

still okay, and you'll have your eyes shut most of the time, won't you?"

"I know, but it's comforting to have a light on when I open them again, and what if that one goes out too?"

"If that light is out when I open my eyes, I'll run yelling and screaming down the stairs, especially if the door is locked," said Gertrude.

Jim and Mary Ann laughed. "Not if the door is locked you won't!" said Jim.

"Well, I'll yell and scream anyway," she replied. "I don't want to be up here in the dark."

"Where're we going to sit? There's not anywhere that's very comfortable in here." Mary Ann looked around. The studio's bare wooden floors were not very inviting as a place to do trance work for an hour.

"Perhaps you'll get us some pillows to sit on, would you Jim? We should have thought of those before we came up," said Gertrude.

"No problem." Jim headed back down stairs. He returned presently with several cushions and a blanket. "Now this is not an invitation to sleep on the job again, Mary Ann. I want results this time." He quirked an eyebrow at her.

"You got results last time," said Mary Ann.

"And how!" He shuddered. "If you girls are ready, I'll leave you to it. Yell if you need anything. I think I'm going to spend some time out here on the landing so I can hear you if you do yell."

"Thanks," said Mary Ann, "We'd really appreciate that. This room has such a dark aura it's hard to stay here for any length of time."

Jim went out closing the door behind himself, and Gertrude and Mary Ann settled themselves as comfortably as possible on the floor. "See you in dreamland." Mary Ann closed her eyes. "I hope this is the last time that I have to trance this room." She altered her attention and was soon drifting away.

Gertrude propped herself in a corner with her cushion and a blanket. I hope so too, this floor is awfully hard, she thought. A ghostly chuckle echoed across her mind. And I'm not even in trance yet, she thought.

She focused her attention inwardly, and was soon seeing the history of the attic. She saw the house as it had been originally, a two room building, solidly built. She watched as each room was added, the building growing upward and outward with each successive addition. They were good carpenters, however lazy they may have been, she thought. The scenes unfolded behind her eyes. She saw Lyman hanging from the rafters, and watched as he exited his body. She watched as the family discovered his rotting corpse in the spring. The attic became silent for a moment as the years reeled by, the only room in the house that was psychically quiet for long periods. I guess they didn't come up here to fight, she thought.

The scene shifted again. Carpenters appeared and work began as the attic was turned into the studio. Willie was everywhere as work progressed. He was accompanied by a woman who was a stranger to Gertrude. That must be his first wife, she thought, as the scene slid quietly past her eyes.

The carpenters faded and the room seemed to darken as Willie began working there. Chaos broke forth in the ether as the strange woman and Willie confronted each other. Then for a time all was still. Willie worked by himself creating huge paintings with angry slashes of the brush and hard raging colours. Laughter echoed through the attic studio, a manic, ugly sound. Willie turned and looked directly at Gertrude. "So you think you can fix things, do you?" he asked quite clearly. He stared at her briefly then returned to his work.

Gertrude cringed psychically at the malevolence of the stare. Her trance began to fade and she forced herself to refocus.

Presently the door opened and Connie appeared, looking like the child she had been when she'd first come there. Her thick blond braid was much shorter, and she was plumper than Gertrude knew her. She posed for Willie, turning her child-like nakedness this way and that until he was satisfied with her posture. He began to paint.

Why, that's the mural in the new courthouse, thought Gertrude. The scene shifted again.

Connie reappeared at the door of the studio and knocked timidly. She was thinner than before, and quite pale. Her hair was much longer. Willie looked up from his work. He said something that Gertrude couldn't hear. Connie seemed to shrink at his words. Willie came toward her and she cringed. He grabbed her braid and she cried out in pain, the cry echoing across Gertrude's consciousness. He pushed her away, and she stumbled hurriedly from the studio.

Gertrude was appalled. So that's what's been going on! I

wonder if that's what she's been afraid to tell us? she thought.

The studio became darker still, and Willie disappeared. A blackness gathered itself in the corner. The shape was familiar. The noise began to grow and expand and take over the studio. As it reached its peak the black shape began to move toward Gertrude. She watched in horror as it seemed to engulf her. The stale and musty smell of it made her want to retch. She screamed and came abruptly out of trance, her eyes large with the terror of her experience.

At Gertrude's scream, Mary Ann joined her in the physical. "Wow!" she said. "That was some event. Let's get out of here." She jumped to her feet.

"You could see it?" Gertrude scrambled upright. "Why didn't you help me?"

"I couldn't. The thing wouldn't let me move." They hurried out the door where Jim met them on the stairs.

"What happened? I heard you scream all the way down to the kitchen."

"Let's get out of here first and then I'll tell you," said Gertrude. "That was horrible!" She shook her head as if she could clear her mind of the horror. "We need to get Molly onto this right away."

"Why weren't you on the landing like you said you'd be?" demanded Mary Ann. They settled themselves around the patio table in the greenhouse. It was still lamp-lit, but a thin, pale light outlined the horizon. "We needed you, and you weren't there." She shuddered at the memory of her psychic helplessness at her friend's danger.

Jim looked at his two helpers unhappily. "I'm truly sorry. Everything had been very quiet for the whole hour, and it was getting to be near the time to wake you up, and I thought you might like something warm to drink when you came around, so I went down to make us a fresh pot of coffee. I was only gone for a couple of minutes."

"Well it was a couple of minutes too long," said Gertrude in strained tones. "I've never been so scared! I thought that thing was going to get me." She still trembled at the memory. "Not only that, Willie was there too and spoke to me. He was kind of threatening. He said: 'So you think you can fix it.'"

Jim reached over and patted her tightly folded hands and was surprised at the coldness of them. "You're in shock!" he said. "You're just freezing." He pulled the blanket from Connie's makeshift bed and wrapped it around her shoulders. "Sit tight and I'll be back in a minute with that coffee." He hurried off to the kitchen.

"Not a word about whether I'm in shock," said Mary Ann after he'd gone. "I'm not, of course, but I could've been." She chuckled, her good spirits having returned.

Jim came back with the coffee and placed a cup in Gertrude's cold hands. "Mm, that feels so good," she said.

"So what did happen up there?" asked Jim.

"I was almost taken over by a darkness," said Gertrude. "It may have been Willie except that he was there too and actually spoke to me. I don't know what the blob's intentions were." She sipped at her steaming coffee.

"And I couldn't do a thing to help her." said Mary Ann. "It was like I was paralysed. I've never felt so helpless. And the thing just laughed."

"Was that the noise I heard as I came up the stairs?"

"I expect it was," said Mary Ann. She sipped her coffee and thought for a moment. "You know, that shape had something very familiar about it."

Gertrude tried to recall the look of it calmly. "I think you're right," she said. "I can't quite put my finger on it though." She recalled how it had seemed to gather from nowhere and begin to come toward her. "The smell was terrible too," she said.

"I know where I've seen that shape before!" Mary Ann fairly danced in her excitement. "It was in the master bedroom. That's the thing that nearly overwhelmed me there. It smelled like that too."

Jim set his cup down abruptly. It splashed. "Are you sure?"

"I'm sure," said Mary Ann. "I'll never forget that smell!" She wrinkled her nose in distaste.

The coffee spread its way slowly toward the wedding pictures still strewn over the table. Gertrude picked them up and dropped a napkin from the replenished supply in the holder onto the coffee to contain it. She glanced absently at the pictures in her hand, and suddenly gasped.

"What's the matter?" asked Mary Ann.

"Are you all right?" asked Jim, at the same time.

"I'm fine," she said, "but look at these pictures, Mary Ann. Doesn't the shape resemble that?" She pointed at the likeness of Willie.

"D'you know, you're right." Mary Ann examined the pictures more closely. "D'you suppose that he's the one who's haunting the attic?"

"But he's not dead yet," said Jim.

"No," agreed Gertrude, "but he might as well be. Remember Molly and her astral travelling trick, and how she nearly drove me crazy before she died."

"D'you suppose it's the same thing?" asked Mary Ann.

"It could be, I guess," said Jim.

"I think it must be," said Gertrude. "I think the whole history of the attic showed itself to me up there, right from the day it was built, including Lyman hanging himself. It was the quietest room that we've listened in, until Willie took over. Then it just seemed to go slowly crazy."

"What else did you see?" asked Jim.

"I saw Willie with Marie, the first Mrs. Poste," said Mary Ann. "At least I think that's who it was, though I couldn't see her clearly. She was about the right size and colouring, but of course she was much younger."

"Is that who that was?" said Gertrude, "I've never seen her, so I wouldn't know."

"Was Connie there?" asked Jim.

"Yes, but she was much younger," said Gertrude. "I think it must have been impressions of when she first came here.

She was posing nude for that big mural downtown."

Jim shook his head. "I wish I knew how you two can do that. It just fascinates me."

"What does?" asked Gertrude.

"Being able to see things like that. What does it look like to you, and how do you know what you're really seeing?"

Gertrude shrugged and looked at Mary Ann. "It looks a little like watching television except that you're right there but not part of it. It's a little gauzy sometimes, but other times it's as clear as watching you sit right there."

"Did you see anything else?"

Gertrude shrugged. "Just that terrible shadow."

"What was that like?"

"It just seemed to be as if all the darkness in the room accumulated in the one spot and formed itself into that lumpy, bulky shape. I really panicked when it started to come toward me!"

"So did I," said Mary Ann. "And I couldn't even help you. It was like whatever it was, kept me from moving."

"So you saw it too?" said Jim.

"Yeah, and I wish I hadn't. It was a thing straight out of a nightmare."

"Well, I guess that's all we can do here tonight," said Jim. "The sun's nearly up, and I hear a car in the lane."

"It's probably Don coming to see if the ghosties got you," said Mary Ann.

The house suddenly became active again, as a tired and drooping Connie came around the corner. She looked up as Jim opened the greenhouse door for her. "Oh, you're still here, are you?" She slumped on the couch and pulled her knees up under her chin.

"Would you like something to eat?" asked Jim.

Connie looked at him dully. "That would be nice," she said, and retreated into herself once more.

"You've had a difficult night of it?" asked Gertrude as she brought her blanket over and wrapped it around Connie.

A tear found its way over the edge of Connie's lashes and rolled down her cheek. "You might say that," she whispered.

Gertrude put her arms around her in comfort. She drew a deep breath, not knowing what to say to Connie. She suddenly stopped, catching a faint stale and musty door emanating from Connie. She sniffed again. She wasn't imagining things. "Connie, what kind of perfume are you wearing?" she asked.

"I'm not wearing any," replied Connie, "why do you ask?"

"I can smell a faint musty smell from you, and I was just wondering."

"Oh, that's probably off Willie. He always smelled as if he hadn't washed for a week. His room at the hospital smells like that too."

Gertrude and Mary Ann exchanged significant glances as Jim returned with a sandwich and a glass of milk for Connie.

"What's up?" he asked as he set the tray down in Connie's lap. "How's Willie?"

"Still with us," said Connie, "though I thought he was gone several times. They had to resuscitate him twice before I got there, they said. He's sleeping now." She took a bite of sandwich and munched it tiredly.

"We're about finished here for the evening. All I have to do is collect up my tape recorders and we can clear out and let you sleep. You look exhausted."

"Yeah, a night in the hospital will do that to you," said Connie.

Jim gathered his equipment and arranged for a meeting with Gertrude and Mary Ann for the evening.

"Will you be all right by yourself?" he asked Connie.

"I have been so far." She drank the last of her milk. "Thanks for the lunch," she said. "I really do appreciate it."

"I know," said Jim.

CHAPTER ELEVEN

On the other side, Molly and Lucy had their hands full. Willie had matured to the age of an adult in terms of his mental skills, but had remained a spoiled child in his behaviour. It had taken a visit from Larry to convince him to stay away from the gates to eternity.

"I wish we could still leash him." Molly smoothed the folds of her bright orange caftan and enjoyed the feel of the material beneath her fingers. "That was so convenient. All we had to do to make him mind was to give it a little twitch and he'd behave like a dream." She watched as Willie went through his daily routine of sit-ups. "Too bad those things won't do him any good in the physical, he could stand to lose a few pounds."

Lucy smiled tiredly. "I sometimes think you're a bit

sadistic, Molly," she said. "A little twitch, indeed!" She leaned her back against the birch tree they were sitting under. "I'm exhausted. I'll be glad when this project is over and we can send him back. I never thought when I agreed to mother him that it would be so tiresome."

"Yes," said Molly, "I've been thankful many times that I'm not the motherly type." She watched Willie scramble to his feet and begin jogging down the hill. "You know, there's something not right about him yet. There's something missing."

"I know. I've been trying to figure it out too. I feel as if we haven't been able to get to the essence of him and effect a change, and his behaviour certainly hasn't improved much since he's been here."

"Yeah, I think the only reason he listens to us is because he doesn't know when Larry might appear and he's a little bit afraid of him." Molly rolled onto her back and looked up at the sky. "I wonder if there's any way we can determine what we might do to complete him?"

Lucy sighed. "I don't know. I've never heard of anything. We just sort of go on intuition around here. Larry might know."

"Larry might know a lot of things," said Molly, "but he's never here."

"Now Molly, this was our project, and Larry has other more important things to do," said Lucy.

"You always stick up for him," said Molly. "We're his protégées so to speak, and he never even checks up on us."

"But we don't know that. He might be looking in on us every evening and just not making himself known. I figure we must be doing all right, or he'd be in here correcting us."

"Well, we could use a little of his wisdom now, before this guy gets sent back," Molly said. "It must be nearly time for that to happen. He can't stay in a coma forever."

"No, he can't." Larry floated in to sit beside Molly. "You're right, it is nearly time for him to go back." He took off his Gainsborough hat and smoothed the voluminous red feather.

"You needn't scare a body to death!" snapped Molly.

Larry chuckled. "Considering that you're already dead, that would be rather difficult." He set the hat on the grass beside himself.

"Where've you been all this time?" asked Molly. "We could've used your help sometimes."

"Meetings," said Larry, "and you didn't need my help, you only thought you did. You got along quite nicely without me."

"Be that as it may, we could use some input now," said Lucy. "Molly and I were just saying how there seems to be something missing in Willie, and we can't quite identify it."

Larry looked down the hill to where Willie was sitting on the edge of the brook cooling his feet in the water. "I see what you mean. His aura is still kind of grey and greasy-looking." Willie began pulling the heads off flowers and throwing them in the brook. "His behaviour leaves something to be desired too."

"You have been keeping track of us," squealed Lucy. "We thought you'd abandoned us, we hadn't seen you in so long."

"Of course. I looked in on you every evening."

"Hooray!" said Molly. "And here I thought I'd lost you forever."

"No such luck." Larry smiled slightly. "Remember, you and I are joined at the hip for the next five hundred years at least. We're partners until one or the other of us decides to reincarnate, and since you can't reincarnate for at least that long, and I don't plan to for longer than that, you're stuck with me."

"Oh?" said Molly. "And what if I don't want to?"

"As a returning spirit you don't have any choice, and since I asked for you, no one else will claim you until I release you from our relationship."

Molly glared at Larry and was about to argue when Lucy shouted: "STOP! WILLIE! STOP!"

Larry and Molly scrambled to their feet and looked to see what Willie was doing. "Darn his hide with a twelve gauge needle," said Molly, "he's messing around at the gate again!"

"WILLIE! GET AWAY FROM THERE!" shouted Larry.

Willie's hand froze on the latch. He turned and looked slyly out the corner of his eye at Larry. "Only fooling." He smirked. "Have to keep you guys on your toes."

Larry shook his head. "We have to get him out of here soon. He's getting too difficult for our resources. The next thing you know he'll be up to something serious and land himself in solitary and then we'd be stuck with him for a long time."

"I hate to send him back the way he is right now." Lucy

frowned. "We really haven't been able to do very much for him."

"Too contrary," said Molly.

"I don't think it's that," said Lucy. "Like I said before, I think he's missing something. He doesn't seem to be quite all there. There's some part of him that we can't reach."

"That's easy enough to discover," said Larry. "We'll just x-ray him."

"X-ray him?" Molly settled her yellow sequined turban more firmly on her head. "If it was as easy as that, why didn't you tell us before?"

"Because I didn't know he needed it," said Larry.

"Because you weren't here," said Molly.

"I was so here," said Larry. "You just didn't see me."

"Will you two stop it," said Lucy. "We'll never get anywhere with this case if you keep fighting like this."

"You're right, Lucy," said Larry. "It's not worth fighting over."

"Says you," muttered Molly. She folded her arms across her chest and half turned away from Larry.

"Tell us about the x-rays, Larry," said Lucy. "Are they really x-rays like in the physical?"

Larry hitched his broad shoulders and turned slightly away from Molly too. "They're similar, only they take pictures of the spirit, since all of the trouble that humans get into originates there in one form or another."

"Where do we take him to get these done?"

"Just into the health centre there. It only takes about five minutes to do the actual exposure. It takes quite a long time to get them positioned correctly and fastened down so they can't move."

"What's it like?" Willie had wandered over and was sitting in the grass just out of arm's reach of any of them.

Larry looked at him in surprise, not having expected to hear from him. "You have to lie very still, son, and a big machine scans your whole body."

"Oh," said Willie. He was quiet for a moment. "Nobody's called me son since my daddy did." Tears formed in his eyes and began to trickle down his face. "My daddy was a good man, but he was no match for mother. I loved my daddy, but he couldn't help me." Willie had reverted back to childhood again.

Larry got up from his seat under the birch tree, put his hat on and arranged the red feather just so. "I guess if we're going to x-ray him, we'd better get to it while he's amenable." He took Willie by the hand and helped him to his feet. "Come on, son, we'll go now and get that test done. It won't hurt a bit."

"Yes, Daddy," said Willie, and trotted off hand in hand with Larry. Lucy and Molly followed at a little distance.

For once Willie was cooperative, and the procedure went smoothly. What they saw made even Larry gasp.

"Well, I've never seen anything quite like this before," he said. "There's a whole chunk missing." He tapped his chin thoughtfully.

"I wonder where it is?" said Lucy. "How could he have gotten over here without all of his spiritual belongings?"

"Humph!" said Molly. "Leave it to Willie to pull a stunt like this. I'll bet he's haunting someone."

"Whatever he's doing, we have to locate the rest of his spirit and get him back together," said Larry. "Where'd he come from?"

"From Charlottetown. It shouldn't be hard to find out the address for sure. It's our old stomping ground. Molly can drop in on Gertrude this evening."

"If I can find her," said Molly. "She's hardly ever home

since she's taken that job with Jim what's-his-name, the ghost hunter. Anyway, I haven't had time to talk to her lately, what with looking after Wee Willie here. She did say that she thought we might be looking after the same situation. The names were the same and the occupation was the same."

"D'you know who it was?" asked Larry.

"That artist guy, I think. She said his name is Willie. She was in a studio of some sort when she called me. I couldn't stay long. Junior here was misbehaving as usual, and Lucy needed my help since you weren't available."

Larry glared at her. "Wasn't Willie an artist?" he asked Lucy.

"I believe he was." She thought for a moment. "I'm sure it is the same guy," she said. "Let's ask him and see if he remembers where he lived in the physical."

Willie was busy tearing the pages out of the "Heavenly Gazette," and didn't look as if he knew anything much at all.

Larry looked at him and shook his head. "He probably doesn't remember."

"It's worth a try, at least," said Lucy. "Ask him anyway, and see what he says."

Larry knelt down in front of Willie and took the magazine from his hands. "Willie, do you remember where you lived before?" he asked.

"WANT MY BOOK!" screamed Willie, reaching for his magazine.

Larry quelled the urge to smack him. "You can have your book in a minute, when you've answered my question."

"Want it now," said Willie. He stomped his foot on the floor.

"In a minute," said Larry. "Do you remember where you used to live?"

Willie looked at Larry slyly. "In a big house," he replied, "with lots of windows. Now can I have my book?"

Larry sighed and handed him back his magazine. "I guess he doesn't remember."

"On the Everly Road," said Willie suddenly. "Want to go back and see Connie." He jumped off the chair and made a race for the door.

"Catch him!" cried Lucy as she went after him as fast as she could float.

Molly stuck out her foot and tripped him as he ran past her. Larry grabbed him by the collar as he went down. "Ow!

You're hurting me!" said Willie from his place on the floor.

"I'll hurt you worse than this," said Larry, "if you don't learn to stay put!" He helped Willie to his feet again and shoved him onto a chair. "Now sit there until I say you can get up," roared Larry.

"Yes, sir," said Willie. "May I have my book, please?"

"NO! Now be quiet!" Larry turned to Molly and Lucy. "Is this what you've been contending with all this time?"

"Yes," said Molly, "as you'd have known if you'd thought to stop by once in a while."

"Every time I was here everything was quiet," said Larry. "You should have called me."

"We did," said Lucy, "but there was never any answer. I thought you had something else more important to do."

Larry sighed, thinking of the gatherings he'd been attending lately. "No," he said, "not as important as this."

"What are we going to do with him?" asked Lucy. "He has to go back soon and we really haven't been able to do very much with him despite all the mothering."

"You were on the right track, but with that big piece of his spirit missing, you'd never have succeeded no matter what you did. As it is we'll have to try and retrieve it and see if we can do anything with it. It'll be as filthy as he was when he first came over."

"Oh, yuck!" said Molly. "D'you mean we'll have to go through all that again?"

"Even if we do find it, how're we going to get it back here?" asked Lucy.

"Find it first and see what condition it's in, then we'll figure out a way to get it back," said Larry. "Now, what I want you to do, is to contact Gertrude and to be sure we have the right haunting. I'll stay here with Lucy and help her ride herd on Willie."

"D'you hear that, Willie?" said Molly, "Larry's going to babysit you."

"All right, Aunt Molly," said Willie, "I'll be good."

"Humph!" said Molly. "You'd better be." She turned to leave. "Aunt indeed!" she muttered as she went out the door.

Jim spent his afternoon listening to tapes. This is probably an exercise in futility, he thought as he turned the first one on. I don't know where people get such wacky ideas. The tape rolled on in silence for several minutes. This is not working, thought Jim, just as the faint sound of sobbing broke through. He sat up abruptly and turned up the volume. Well! Well! Maybe I'm wrong. A babble of voices drowned out the sobbing, no one voice clearer than any other.

After ten minutes he heard Gertrude and Mary Ann enter the room and announce themselves. They discussed where they were going to sit and presently they were quiet. The noise on the tape grew louder. Jim strained to hear. An argument broke out and he heard distinctly the name 'Georgie' spoken in angry tones, followed by a crash. Sounds of a party became prominent, and the name 'Gus' came through, answered by a child's piping voice. He heard himself come quietly into the room to switch the tapes to continue the recording. As Gertrude and Mary Ann came out of trance the noise diminished in intensity. This is a great deal more than I was expecting, he thought to himself as he changed tapes. The girls will be very interested to hear this.

The other tapes were of a similar nature. The tape from the studio was the most useful. It had recorded a man's menacing laughter and Gertrude's scream which had been reproduced exactly as Jim remembered it. At the sound,

Betsy roused from her slumbers beside the stove and woofed.

"It's okay Betsy, go back to sleep. It's only a tape," said Jim. Betsy lay down again with a deep, doggy whine.

That evening the team listened attentively as Jim played the tapes for them. "To save us time, I've selected what I think are the most useful parts," said Jim. He inserted a tape. "I think the one from the studio is the most interesting. You can actually hear scraps of conversation on it."

He pushed the button to roll the tape and advanced it to a few minutes after Gertrude and Mary Ann had come in and settled themselves. A man's voice broke through quite clearly. "You'll do no such thing, you silly bitch!" he said. "Now, get out of my sight!" A door slammed loudly. Everyone in the kitchen jumped. In a few minutes the voice continued, "Not that way! Don't you know anything? Move over! Not there! There! What's the matter with you? Are you stupid or something?!" A few minutes of silence followed this outburst. Presently it was terminated by laughter and Gertrude's scream.

"What happened? What was that?" asked Don.

"It was nothing," said Gertrude. "I just saw a dark shadow and it startled me momentarily, that's all."

"So what do you guys think?" Jim smiled. "Kind of interesting, eh? I'm glad I thought of doing that."

"It's curious how the sounds increased when we went into trance," said Gertrude.

"We must have supplemented the available energy." Mary Ann propped her feet on the open oven door. There was still a residue of heat left from suppertime. "It's no wonder we were tired when we finished."

"Could you hear any conversation in the studio when you were in trance?" asked Gertrude.

"Not really. I mostly just got the tones of voice and the feelings the conversation generated. Willie's a nasty man."

"He is a nasty man," said Jim. "The more I learn about him, the less I like him."

"I wonder if that conversation really took place," said Don. "Maybe this is all just a product of your minds."

"Oh, it took place all right," said Mary Ann. "Anything that strongly imprinted on the ether had to have happened."

Gertrude shifted in her chair. "My goodness I'm sleepy! What did you put in the coffee, Jim?"

"Just coffee, my dear. Why? Is it not strong enough for you?"

At that moment a series of knocks sounded on the mantle shelf. Everyone's head turned at once to the source. Gertrude yawned; her eyelids drooped. "I wonder if that's for me?" She allowed herself to drift off into trance.

"Took you long enough," snapped Molly from her seat beside the clock. "I've been trying to get your attention for the last ten minutes."

"Sorry," said Gertrude. "I wasn't paying any attention. Besides, how was I to know? I've been trying to contact you for weeks now, and you haven't responded, and we've never set up a signal for when you want me."

"You're excused this time, but the next time, pay attention." Molly ignored her own neglect of Gertrude.

"So what did you want me for?"

"It seems we have a problem. I understand that you've been investigating a case of haunting out on the Everly Road at Willie Poste's."

"Yes, and not having very much luck with it either. We sure could've used your help on this one."

"What seems to be the problem there?"

"Well, it doesn't act like a true haunting. There have been no sightings of ghostly figures, and the events are much too real to be attributed to ghosts. It's more like a poltergeist than a ghost, except that it doesn't act like a true poltergeist either. Willie had a fall about a month ago now, and has been in a coma ever since. His wife is terrified, and the house has been unlivable from the noise this past week or so."

"Your problem and my problem are one and the same."

"Oh?" said Gertrude. "How's that?"

"Willie said he lived on the Everly Road and that he wanted to go and see Connie."

"Willie Poste's wife's name is Connie so we do have a common problem." Gertrude thought for a few moments. "But I thought mortals couldn't haunt."

"They can't technically, but Willie's a special case. He's been over here getting fixed since his fall. He's about ready to be sent back but we can't find a piece of his spirit. We think it may be still at his home."

"Well, that would certainly explain all that's been happening here," said Gertrude. "What's he like over there?"

"Hell on wheels!" snapped Molly. "I've had to literally sit on him a few times, and poor Lucy is exhausted. The only one he pays any attention to is Larry."

"So he's not much different from when he's here, is he?"

Molly shook her turbaned head. "If he's this bad at home, it's a wonder he has any friends left."

"He doesn't," said Gertrude, "and his little wife is long-suffering." She recounted to Molly some of what they'd learned about Willie.

"Humph!" said Molly. "I guess we were lucky to get off so easily."

"So what can I do for you?"

"I need you to help me find the missing piece and package it up for transport."

"I think I know where it is, so that part's easy enough. Can I bring Mary Ann along?"

"The more the merrier," said Molly. "The quicker we put Wee Willie back together again, the quicker we'll be rid of him."

"Let's go then," said Gertrude, "I'll call you when I get there." She surfaced quickly from her trance.

"That was Molly." She stretched and yawned. "She needs our help."

"I don't think we have time to help her right now," said Jim. "Not with all the work we still have to do out at Willie's."

"I think she may have just given us the answer to the events out at Willie's," said Gertrude. She told them about her conversation with Molly.

"Hm, that is an interesting development," said Jim. "Well, I guess one more night won't hurt, and it may even help. Let's go."

A half hour later they were knocking on the greenhouse door. Connie sprang from her couch to let them in. There were traces of tears on her cheeks and dark circles of fatigue beneath her eyes. "What's the matter?" she asked.

"I think we may have had a breakthrough," said Jim. "In fact I'm pretty sure we do. D'you mind if Gertrude and Mary Ann go up to the studio for a little while?"

"No, of course not. I was hoping you'd come by this evening. It's been very noisy up there all day. Noisier than usual, and during the daylight too."

"Go ahead, then, girls. I'm going to trust in your good judgement. If you want to go and wait on the landing, Don, go ahead too. Just don't get in the way."

The three friends wended their way up to the attic. The noise was deafening. Don perched on the top step determined not to interfere. His expression was very worried. "You'll scream if you need help, won't you?" he said to them.

"Of course." Mary Ann chuckled. "I'm the biggest chicken on Prince Edward Island, so if Gertrude doesn't scream, I certainly will."

Gertrude and Mary Ann went into the studio and closed the door.

"I guess the first thing to do is to contact Molly and let her know where to come," said Gertrude. She sat down on the pillows left from the previous night.

"Do you want me to trance with you?" asked Mary Ann.

"I think so," said Gertrude. "I may need your help." She shifted her attention inward, and began calling for Molly. The room was as dark as ever. Presently Mary Ann was with her. Together they called for Molly.

"She's taking a long time coming," said Mary Ann. "I wonder if our signal's faint or something."

"It may be this room," said Gertrude. "It feels as thick as cotton wool in here tonight. I can hardly breathe."

The blackness grew more intense. Raucous laughter filled the ether. "MOLLY! MOLLY!" called Gertrude and Mary Ann in unison.

"Maybe we need to go out on the lawn and call her," said Mary Ann. "The ether will be clear out there and then maybe she'll be able to hear us."

Gertrude projected her astral self out to the front lawn and called again. This time Molly answered.

"Took you long enough," she grumbled. "I was beginning to think you'd deserted me."

"Never!" Gertrude laughed. "That room up there is pretty dense. I had a hard time calling you." They wafted gently upward to the studio.

"Phew!" said Molly. "What a mess! Where's Willie?"

"I'm not sure," said Gertrude. "This is where we heard his voice, and this is the most active room in the house right now, so I figured he'd be here."

Molly looked more closely at her surroundings. "He can't be far. I can smell him."

Gertrude sniffed. "Is that what we've been smelling all these times when we've been here?"

"You betcha," said Molly. "We got him cleaned up a little on the other side so he doesn't smell so bad there, but we sure had a hard time keeping him out of eternity."

"I didn't know you could do that," said Mary Ann.

"I always thought that if you were dead you were dead. That there was no coming back once you were truly on the other side."

"Usually that's the way it is." Molly sniffed the air again. "In Willie's case he could come back again and make amends for all the bad things he's done because all the people that he's done them to are still in the physical. So we've been trying to rehabilitate him, so to speak, on the other side. We have a facility there to accommodate special cases like him without contaminating eternity with them. Besides, he never really got to the other side as such. We never let him get through the gates."

She ran her hand over the counter top. "Oh, yuck! What's this mess?" She wiped her hand in a fold of her caftan. The black goo wouldn't wipe off. She held her hand up to her nose and sniffed at it. "Phew! It smells like Willie." She peered more closely at her surroundings. "This place is covered in the stuff." A mocking laugh rang through the room.

Gertrude and Mary Ann looked at one another. "I think you've just found Willie," said Gertrude.

"Oh, the disgusting little skunk!" raged Molly. "He's

gone and spread himself around so we can't catch him!" She thought for a moment, then a cunning look came over her face. "Have you got a vacuum cleaner?" she asked.

"I think I saw one downstairs," said Gertrude.

"It's in the hall closet," said Mary Ann. "I'll go and get it." She shifted her focus to the physical, and was soon on her way down to fetch the vacuum cleaner.

"What's going on in there?" asked Don as she passed him on the landing on her way back.

"We've found Willie. Now we've got to get him."

"With a vacuum cleaner?"

Mary Ann closed the door behind her, leaving Don on the other side, shaking his head in wonder.

"I'll just take the essence of this machine to suck up the essence of Willie," Molly said, as Mary Ann returned. "Plug it in. I'll need to use the energy field created by the flow of electricity in the physical to run it."

Mary Ann plugged in the machine and it sprang to life. As Molly approached with the dusting attachment, the black goo began to quiver. She applied the nozzle to as many surfaces as she could reach, the blackness that was Willie running ahead of her and finding its way into cracks and corners in its effort to escape the monster vacuum. "I'll have to use the crevice tool now," she said, detaching the dusting tool. "He's slid into the corners and I can't get the rest of him without it."

The crevice tool was long and narrow. "Here Willie, Willie," called Molly. She suctioned out the corners of the room. "Come to Auntie Molly. It'll be easier if you come quietly, you know. There's a good boy."

At last Willie was contained in the belly of the vacuum cleaner. "What do we do with him now?" asked Gertrude.

Molly grinned. "Have you got a baggie?"

Gertrude sent Mary Ann off to fetch some plastic bags. "What's happening in there now?" asked Don. "Where're you going?"

"To get some bags." Mary Ann hurried downstairs. She returned in a few minutes with a couple of small garbage bags. "I hope these are all right." She eased past Don. "It's all I could find."

"What're you going to do with those?" asked Don to the closing door.

"These are all I could find." Mary Ann took a moment to catch her breath. "I hope it's all right." She dropped the bags on the counter, and opened them out. They immediately disappeared.

"Now you be right ready to pull the bag over the top of the machine when I pull the lid off," said Molly to Gertrude. "I don't want him to escape." She unfastened the clips that held the lid in place. "Are you ready now? One, two, three," and the transfer was made.

"I think I'd better double bag him before I try to move him," said Molly. The commotion inside the bag made Gertrude fear for its longevity. Molly flipped another bag over the first one, and tied it off with a twist tie.

"You ladies have been a great deal of help this evening." Molly gave a heave to the bag. It barely moved. "Mercy, he's heavy! I hope I can lift him all by myself." She gave another heave. "I may have to get Larry to help me after all."

Gertrude looked around the studio and spied a backpack in the corner. "Will this do?" She retrieved its essence from under the counter and brushed the dust off.

"That may be just the ticket," said Molly. She wrestled Willie into the pack and hoisted him onto her back. "I'll see you later, and thanks." She faded from sight.

With Willie's departure on Molly's back, the room

brightened. "It sure smells better in here." Mary Ann sniffed the air as Gertrude came out of trance.

"It's considerably quieter, too," said Gertrude. She yawned and straightened her shoulders. "This has been a good night's work."

CHAPTER TWELVE

M olly struggled with her heavy burden all the way back. The large fragment of Willie's spirit fought her every inch of the way. She arrived at the daisy field and dropped the backpack with a thump at Larry's feet. It bounced once and then lay still.

"Good job, Molly," said Larry, "but we'll have to be more gentle with him than that, or we won't be able to tell the bruises from the dirt."

"What's that?" asked Willie He poked the backpack with his foot. The bag moved. "Oh!" Willie jumped back. "It's alive!"

"Unfortunately." Molly raised an eyebrow.

"It belongs to you, Willie," said Lucy. She glared at Molly.

"Something to play with?" asked Willie. He was still in his child mode.

"Well, you can't play without it." Molly ignored Lucy's glare.

"Can I play with it now?" asked Willie.

"Not now," said Larry, "it goes inside you."

"I WANT IT NOW!" screamed Willie, throwing a major tantrum.

The other three exchanged glances. "Not now," said Larry to Willie.

"NOW!" Willie, dropped to the ground and began kicking his heels.

"I think we'd better schedule him for psychic surgery immediately," said Larry.

"The sooner the better." Molly watched Willie's antics out the corner of her eye.

"What will they do to him?" asked Lucy.

Larry shrugged. "You know, the usual surgery stuff. Open him up and replace the part, and put him back together. Of course they'll have to clean the piece first or Willie'll be almost as bad as ever when we send him back."

"All that without anaesthetic, I hope," said Molly.

"Molly! You don't really mean that." Lucy was shocked. "He's not that bad, and even if he was, he wouldn't deserve that."

"No, of course I don't really mean it," said Molly. "I was just venting."

"Psychic surgery doesn't hurt anyway," said Larry, "though they'll be lucky if they can hold this character down long enough to do anything."

Willie had exhausted his tantrum and fallen asleep where he lay. Larry nudged him gently with his toe. "C'mon Willie, it's time to go and be put back together again."

"Don't want to," muttered Willie, and rolled over.

Larry grabbed him by the hand and hoisted him to his feet. "Now I thought you knew better than to disagree with me." He dragged the reluctant Willie toward the health centre. Molly and Lucy followed behind them lugging the heavy backpack between them.

The door to the health centre stood open to let in the evening breeze. Willie figured out their destination just as they were going through the door and screamed: "NO!" He grabbed onto the door jamb.

"YES!" said Larry with equal determination. He pried

Willie's fingers loose one by one.

"Why don't you want to?" asked Lucy. "You'll feel so much better and then you can go and see Connie."

"Because I don't want to be grown-up," sobbed Willie. "I'm ugly. Everybody hates me." His wails grew louder. His fat body shook with them.

"You don't have to be ugly," said Lucy. "You can be anything you want to be, all you have to do is be it."

Willie's sobs reduced themselves to a few sniffles while he thought this over. "Really?" He wiped his nose on his shirt sleeve. "My other mommy said I was bad and that nothing would make me get better." He sniffed again.

"That's not true." Lucy crossed her fingers behind her back and hoped she wasn't lying. "Now, why don't you get up and go with Uncle Larry. He wants to help you get well."

"Okay." Willie scrambled to his feet and offered his hand to Larry. "Good-bye, Mommy," he called over his shoulder as he walked away. "I love you, Mommy." The treatment room doors closed behind them.

"I sure hope you're right." Molly settled down on the sofa and shuffled through the outdated magazines.

"I hope so too," said Lucy. "I didn't like to lie to him,

but I had to say something or he wouldn't have gone." She sighed deeply. "I suppose I'll have to answer for that one at the next review." She sighed again.

They were silent for awhile. Presently Larry joined them. "We got him immobilized finally," he said. "I didn't think we would for a few minutes."

"He fought, did he?" said Molly.

"Oh, yes," he said, "did you really think he wouldn't?"

"No," agreed Lucy. "If he's nothing else, he is a fighter." She sighed again.

Larry leaned back in his chair and folded his massive arms across his chest. "He's going back as soon as the operation is over, you know."

"Well, that's a relief!" said Molly. "Now we can all get some rest."

"Oh," said Lucy. She was silent for a moment. "I think I'm going to miss him."

"How can you say that?" said Molly. "After all the trouble he's caused us."

"I rather liked the little boy that he was. He was never malicious, only misguided. It was when he was getting toward adulthood that the maliciousness set in."

"And how!" snapped Molly. "All I can say is that I'll be glad to see the back of him."

"Anyway," said Larry, "you'll be able to look in on him from time to time if you want to."

The treatment room doors swung open and Willie entered, attended by the two surgery technicians. "Here he is," said the one nearest to Larry. "It's the best we could do with what you gave us. We couldn't get the piece quite clean. It's still dirtier than the rest even though we soaked it in sea salt." They handed Willie over to Larry and returned to their duties.

"How do you feel?" asked Lucy.

"Pretty good, considering," boomed Willie in an adult voice. "What's for supper?"

"Actually, you'll have to let the doctors decide that," said Larry as he led Willie back to the daisy field. Molly and Lucy followed close behind. "You'll be returning to the physical this evening."

"What's that?" asked Willie

"Back to where you came from," said Larry as they made their way down to the brook.

"How do I get there?"

"Once you cross the brook you'll be on your way."

"I can't get lost?"

"Not even if you tried," said Larry. They reached the edge of the brook. "Well, this is it. You're on your own."

Willie stepped down into the water. "It's cold," he said.

"It's night time," said Larry. "You could've gone over the bridge."

"Now you tell me." Willie waded across.

"Good luck!" called Larry and Lucy.

"Happy landings," shouted Molly. Willie disappeared from view.

At two o'clock in the morning Willie opened his eyes to take in the white walls and glass doors of the I.C.U. His heart monitor blinked steadily above his bed, his I.V. dripped fast enough to keep him hydrated in his comatose state. A feeding tube had been inserted directly into his stomach and the constant flow of nourishment gave him a warm and contented feeling. He looked around, a little disoriented at first. I wonder where Lucy is? he thought. I wonder where I am? Presently a nurse came in to check his vital signs.

"Oh, you're awake, are you?" she said when she saw Willie's eyes open. "They said at report that you were starting to wake up." She wrapped the blood pressure cuff around his arm and pumped it up.

"Ow!" said Willie, "that hurts!" His voice was weak and a little wobbly.

The nurse ignored his complaint. "Can you squeeze my hands?" she asked. Willie squeezed. "That's good," she said. "Let me check your pupils." She flashed her penlight in his eyes. Willie blinked at the sudden brightness. "D'you know what year it is?" she asked. Willie just looked at her. He sighed deeply and closed his eyes.

The nurse completed the neurological check, tidied Willie and his bed and left the room. "He's awake," she said to the other nurse.

"Miracles do occur," she said. "I suppose we'd better let Dr. Stuart and Willie's wife know." She picked up the phone. "You got his vitals?"

The phone rang at Connie's house just as the four friends and colleagues finished their coffee break in the greenhouse.

It was Connie. "He's awake," she said dully.

Jim hung up the phone. "That was Connie. Wee Willie's back in the land of the living."

"I wonder what condition he's in?" Gertrude shivered and stuck her arms into the sleeves of her sweater.

"She didn't say," said Jim.

In about twenty minutes Connie arrived and was perched on the edge of the couch wringing her hands. "I'm sorry for interrupting your work like this, but I had no one else to call on."

"That's just fine, dear." Mary Ann sat down beside Connie and put a motherly arm around Connie's thin shoulders. "We were going to just make one more pass of the house and call it a night anyway."

"You were?"

"We thought perhaps you'd like to know what we found out," said Jim. "It'll help you to sleep better at night, I think."

"Oh," said Connie. "It was nice and quiet here last night. I hope it's nothing too terrible, I don't think I could cope with that." She began playing nervously with her braid.

"Nothing that can hurt you," said Mary Ann. "It's just a lot of psychic noise left over from generations ago."

"It's mostly all old news," said Gertrude.

Jim told her the stories that Jobie and Gus had told him, making them funny and lighthearted. When she laughed out loud in all the right places, they realized that it was the first time they had heard her laugh.

"This is the best I've felt in months." She wiped tears of laughter from her eyes. "But what about Willie?" she asked, suddenly sobering.

"Willie's been taken care of," said Gertrude. "You said he'd awakened from his coma didn't you?"

"Yes, this evening." She jumped up and began to pace the greenhouse floor. "Oh, dear, what am I going to do?" she wailed.

"What do you mean?" asked Gertrude. "Do about what?"

"About Willie," said Connie in anxious tones. "He'll hate me. He'll think I pushed him, and I didn't, and I won't be able to convince him. Oh, what am I going to do?" Tears ran in torrents down her face. She scrubbed at them with the tail of her shirt to no avail.

"Willie probably won't even remember what happened

that close to his fall," said Gertrude.

"D'you think not?" asked Connie. "Maybe he won't punish me, then."

"Anyway, he may never have the strength to harm you again."

Connie didn't look particularly heartened by this news. "I'd so hoped he'd have died," she muttered under her breath.

"What's that you said?" asked Mary Ann, frowning a little in her effort to make sense of what she'd just heard.

Connie repeated herself more loudly. "I'd hoped he'd have died!" A small sob escaped her. "There, I've finally said it out loud."

"My goodness." Mary Ann was quite taken aback with the vehemence of the wish. "But he's your husband!"

"Unfortunately," said Connie sadly, and sniffed. "I think I hate him!"

The others waited quietly. Connie hardly noticed them. "I do hate him," she amended.

"Whatever did he do to make you feel this way?" asked Mary Ann.

Connie stared at the table seeing only into her past.

"What didn't he do," she said.

"Did you push him?" asked Mary Ann.

"No, but I've wished him dead so many times, I might as well have."

"Do you suppose you could tell us about it?"

Connie sighed, a sound that seemed to come from the bottoms of her feet. "I guess I'll have to now," she said. Haltingly, she began to tell a story of deprivations and petty meannesses, of slurs and put downs against her character, a careful and seemingly well-planned execution of her personality, her talents, and her dreams. The telling of it was long and painful. All the while she stared unseeingly at the table in front of her. "The last thing he said to me was that I was an untalented bitch." Her voice dwindled away to nothing. The only sound that could be heard for several minutes was the chirp of a single cricket hidden against the warmth of the foundation. "Maybe I am," she said at last.

"Did he ever beat you?" asked Mary Ann at last.

"Not exactly," said Connie. "He didn't have to. He'd pull me by my hair, and twist my arms behind my back when he wanted to force me to do anything. He knew how to hurt me where it wouldn't show." A new flood of tears rolled down her face and she sniffed deeply, and scrubbed at them with the heel of her hand. "There, now you know everything," she said. She sat down on the couch again, next to Mary Ann and hung her head.

Mary Ann handed her a tissue. "I guess you have good reason to wish him gone," she said. She stroked Connie's down-bent head.

Connie broke forth with a fresh bout of weeping. "I hate him! I just hate him so much!" she exclaimed pounding the couch with her fists. "I'm so afraid of him."

"Do you want to leave here?" asked Mary Ann.

"What's the use? He'd only come and get me," said Connie. "Then I'd really be in for it. Besides, I'm married to him. I can't just leave, he'd have no one to look after him when he gets home from the hospital."

Mary Ann and Gertrude exchanged glances and shook their heads in amazement at Connie's contradictory thoughts.

"It doesn't sound a very healthy relationship," said Mary Ann, "but you know best." She frowned. "You know that you can call us any time and we'll come for you."

"Oh, would you really?" asked Connie.

"Of course," said Mary Ann and Gertrude in unison. "All you have to do is call."

Connie sighed. It was a huge release of tension. "I think I know what I'm going to do now. I'll stay here until Willie gets home and back on his feet. I'll see how he is then, and if he hasn't changed, I'll just leave." Her shoulders slumped again. "If he'll let me," she said.

Jim cleared his throat. "So what exactly happened the night he fell?" he asked.

Connie jumped. She'd forgotten that the others were even there. She turned a dull glance in Jim's direction. "We'd had a terrible fight for the first time in months. I'd given up fighting with him because it wasn't any use to, and that made him mad too, when he couldn't goad me into fighting back. I walked out of his studio and he followed me onto the landing. That's when he told me I was a no-talent. I slapped his face. It was the first time I'd ever retaliated. He lunged for me and I ducked aside and he lost his footing and went down over the stairs. I really didn't push him."

Connie was silent for a long time then, remembering the horror of that night, the fight, the slap still resounding in her ears, the ugly pig face of him coming at her, with its cheap toupee gleaming greenly in the light from the open studio door. She could still hear the thump and clatter of his pudgy body as it rolled and bounced its way down the stairs to fetch up with a sickening crunch against the newel post at the bottom. The silence that had followed was the loudest sound of all.

"I don't understand why he didn't break his neck," she said.

"Well," said Jim, after a few moments. "Well! That's quite a story! Have you told anyone else this?"

Connie struggled to sit up straighter on the couch. It was as if a load had been lifted from her thin shoulders. "D'you mean like the police?"

"Anyone," replied Jim, "a friend, a relative, a counsellor."

"I just told the police that I didn't push him. I can't prove that because I'm the only one who can say anything about what happened that night, so there's no point in trying to argue with them about what happened. The more I'd argue, the more likely they'd be to think it was me, and I didn't do it."

"What about a friend?"

"What friend?" asked Connie. "He didn't allow me to

keep a friend. I was never allowed to leave this property, and if I was out of his sight too long I was 'punished' when I returned. I used to try to take the dog for a walk out back but I always had to pay for it."

Mary Ann was aghast. "Punish you for taking the dog for a walk?"

"Yeah, he'd beat the dog, and send me to bed without supper. Finally the dog ran away. I think he's over at Simpsons' now. I see him sometimes, scouting around the back of the property. He looks good now, he used to be so thin."

"D'you mean he'd actually send you to bed without supper?! How could he do that?"

"By threatening to do worse to the dog. I couldn't bear to see poor Sandy harmed. He was such a gentle creature. He was my friend." Another tear welled up and rolled over her lashes. She sniffed. "I'd rather have gone hungry than to see Sandy go hungry."

Mary Ann put her arms around her. She was shocked to feel Connie's ribs through her shirt. She could hardly bear to ask the next question. "Did you have to go without supper often?" She stroked Connie's blond head.

Connie could only nod. After a few moments she

gulped and said, "Sometimes he'd make me go for several days without food. Especially if he caught me sneaking down to get a bite after he'd forbidden me. I don't know how he knew, but he always seemed to. He'd be in his studio working and all of a sudden he'd be in the kitchen right behind me. He was always doing that. I was a nervous wreck."

"Was he never out of the house so you could get yourself a bite to eat?"

"He finally took to locking the refrigerator door and the cupboards too. I can show you the locks." She smiled grimly. "I found his keys and took the locks off the night they took him out of here in the ambulance. Did I have a feast! I almost made myself sick." She remembered the glorious sense of abundance as she opened packages and cans and ate three things at once, and for the first time in five years went to bed satisfied and full. "I've even gained some weight this last month," she said. The others exchanged glances. Connie was still very thin.

"Didn't you know that he was like this before you married him?"

"Not really. I'd heard rumours, of course, but once I

started modelling for him, he acted as if I were the best thing that had ever happened to him. And, after all, he was a world famous artist. I didn't realize that the reason he wanted me all to himself until we got married was so that no one could tell me anything he'd have to answer for. His first wife is still around and she could have warned me, I suppose. If I'd have listened. It seemed like such a good thing at the time. I had no one, and I was struggling to make ends meet, and here was this wonderful opportunity to be close to a great artist and learn from him. I didn't have any idea that the day before we got married would be the last day I'd paint. We got married in the morning and I guess he must have gone sometime during the night and taken my painting equipment because I never saw it again. I've searched the house over and I never could find it. I still haven't found it!"

"Did you ever think about leaving him?" asked Mary Ann.

"Lots of times, but it would never have worked. He'd have always found me and brought me back. He said once that he'd kill me if I ever left. Besides where would I go?"

"Home to your parents?" said Mary Ann.

"They don't want me. They told me to get out and not come back. So I did."

"Maybe he'll be changed by this experience," said Gertrude.

"He'd have to change an awful lot," said Connie.

The next afternoon Connie paid a visit to the hospital. She was surprised to see how thin Willie had become. He must have been good looking when he was young, she thought. She entered the room.

"Connie!" cried Willie. "Where've you been? I've missed you."

"Missed me?" asked Connie. She approached the bed cautiously.

"Yes, where've you been?" Willie watched her intently.

Connie squirmed. "At home."

"Why'm I here?" asked Willie. "The nurses won't tell me."

"You had a fall," said Connie, "and you banged your head."

"Have you seen Lucy?" Willie continued to gaze intently at Connie.

"Who's Lucy?" Connie frowned slightly.

"You know … Lucy."

Connie shook her head. "I don't know her, is she one of the nurses?"

"I don't think so. She was always with Molly. They lived in a daisy field."

"I think you must have dreamed it," said Connie. "Maybe you should rest now. I'll go and get some coffee for us and come back later." She rose from her chair and hurried away. She returned a half hour later and Willie was napping.

She sat down beside his bed and sipped her coffee waiting for him to awaken. Her eyes drooped and she fell into a light sleep to awaken a few minutes later to find Willie gazing at her. He smiled slightly, and to her astonishment he said, "I'm sorry, Connie. I've been very unkind to you." His expression became very serious. "Can you ever forgive me?"

Connie couldn't answer.

"I'll understand if you can't," said Willie. "I know what I've done. Molly and Lucy showed me that. So if you want to leave …" his voice trailed off. A tear found its way down his whiskered cheek.

Willie crying? That is one for the record, thought Connie. "I don't know, Willie, I'll have to think about it. In the meantime, your coffee's getting cold." She handed him the paper cup.

A few weeks later Jim received a formal invitation to supper at the Poste home. Everyone was to come, including Betsy. At the appointed time they arrived to find a somewhat thinner Willie sitting in the greenhouse.

"Pardon me if I don't get up to greet you," he said, "but I'm still a little weak from my stay in the hospital, and I've had a busy day." He smiled a secret smile. "Find yourselves a place to sit, Connie will be here in a minute with some refreshments."

Chairs scraped over the flagstones of the greenhouse floor as they made themselves comfortable. "So you're feeling much improved, are you?" asked Jim.

"Oh, yes, this is the best I've felt in a very long time. In fact I can't remember when I've felt this good. I can't wait 'til my strength returns enough so that I can take up my painting again."

Connie entered carrying a tray of glasses and finger foods. She had gained a little more weight and seemed happier than the others had expected to find her. "Supper'll be ready in a little while." She set the tray on the table. "I just have to do a few more things."

"We'll help you." Mary Ann jumped to her feet and followed Connie back into the kitchen with Gertrude close behind. "I just love kitchen work," she said.

Gertrude made no pretence about work. "How's Willie been?" she asked as soon as the door closed behind them.

"Better." Connie smiled. "In fact he's a changed man. He's not at all the same old Willie." She began dicing potatoes for the salad.

"So he's not hard to take care of?" asked Mary Ann.

"No," said Connie. "He's always trying to wait on me. I just can't get over the change in him. He even told me where he'd hidden my paints, and he's been encouraging me to work again. I can hardly believe it."

"Has he said anything about his accident?" asked Gertrude.

"Not much. He just said that he'd had some really wild dreams when he was in the coma. Something about two women in a daisy field, and some guy called Larry."

Gertrude and Mary Ann exchanged glances. "That's all he said about his dreams?" asked Mary Ann.

"That's all he's ever told me. By the way, I found out how he always knew when I was in the kitchen before."

"How's that?" asked Mary Ann.

"When I went up to the studio to get my painting supplies where he told me to look, there was a heat duct from the kitchen in the same space. There's a panel in the wall up there that opens into a space beside it, and you can hear everything that goes on down here."

"Simple explanations for simple things," said Mary Ann.

"What do you plan to do?" asked Gertrude.

Connie shrugged. "Stay here, I guess. He's really changed and if he stays as pleasant as this it won't be too bad. Besides, I don't have anywhere else to go." She stirred mayonnaise into the potatoes. "… and I am married to him."

"But what if he doesn't stay pleasant?" asked Mary Ann. "This may just be a symptom of his convalescence, you know."

Connie's face darkened with worry. "I know, and I don't

know what I'll do if that's all it is." She thought for a few moments. "I guess I could always call on Max Perry for a few days. He's the director of the art institute, you know. He was always very kind to me when I was a student there."

"We've met Max," said Gertrude. "I'm sure he'd help you if you needed him to."

"And for more than a few days, too, I think," said Mary Ann. "I was really impressed with the man. He seems very kind."

Connie stirred more mayonnaise into the salad. "Oh, yes, he always was that," she replied. "More like a father than a teacher to me." She began spooning the salad onto the bed of lettuce. "He's the kind of man whom you always treat carefully because it would be so easy to take advantage of him." She sprinkled a little paprika over the top of the salad. "There, I think everything's ready. Do you mind carrying some things into the greenhouse for me, please? It's such a lovely evening that I hate to waste it sitting indoors."

In a few minutes the table was set, and Connie took her place beside Willie and began passing bowls of food. "Everyone just help themselves, I've made lots of everything."

"It all looks so good," said Mary Ann. "You've certainly

gone to a lot of trouble."

"No trouble, really," replied Connie. "I like to cook. I've never had much opportunity before."

"So, Willie, what are you going to do when you're fully recovered?" asked Don.

Willie looked at Connie and smiled. Connie blushed. "I think I'm going to take it easier than I have. You know, look after Connie, paint a little, maybe plant a flower garden. I find that I've taken quite a liking to daisies. I think I might plant the periphery of the lawn with wild flowers."

"And what are you going to do, Connie?" asked Mary Ann.

Connie glanced shyly at Willie. "Willie said that I could go back to art school if I wanted to. I think I may do that. It's wonderful to be painting again."

"Do you have any projects in mind, Willie?" asked Jim.

Willie frowned slightly. "This is going to sound crazy, but since I've come out of coma, I've had this strange urge to paint seascapes. You know, summer seas, not storms. I've always painted energetic abstracts. I don't know how my public will take this sudden change of style."

"You'll probably attract a whole new following," said

Connie. "You're brilliant with paint, so I wouldn't worry about it too much."

"You're the one that's brilliant, my dear," said Willie. He looked at the others. "I could hardly believe my eyes when I saw how her work had matured even for not having painted for so long. She's going to be famous someday."

Connie blushed again. "I'd be happy to just sell a few." Just then a puppy bounced into the greenhouse. It was a miniature Betsy. Connie jumped up and grabbed the squirming animal that licked her face enthusiastically. "Oh, dear," she said nervously, looking at Willie out the corner of her eye, "I'm sorry, I had her locked up in her kennel. She must have gotten out somehow."

"That's all right, my dear," said Willie, "no harm done."

"What's her name?" asked Gertrude.

"Willie suggested that I name her Molly."

Mary Ann tried hard to keep a straight face. Gertrude didn't bother. "That's a wonderful name!" she said.

The next evening the others were all at Jim's house as had become their habit.

"I hope what we saw out at Willie's yesterday evening was a sample of things to come," said Gertrude.

"I think it is," said Don. "I have a feeling the changes are for real and are permanent."

"Did you say you have a feeling?" said Mary Ann. "Have you been developing your psychic powers too?"

Don frowned slightly. "It rubs off."

Gertrude yawned. "I think I'm being summoned," she said, and lapsed into trance.

Molly and Lucy were perched in their usual places, one on either side of the clock on the mantle shelf.

"It's about time you got here," said Molly. "We don't have all night."

"Now Molly," said Lucy, "you know we're on vacation, and we can stay as long as we like this evening."

"And a well-earned one it is, too," said Molly. "That Willie was a handful."

"How's he doing?" asked Lucy.

"He's home," said Gertrude, "and he does seem to be pleasanter. Connie is certainly happier. She's going back to art school, and he's let her have a dog."

"That's good." Lucy smiled. "He's really not so bad,

once you get to know him. What did she name the dog?"

"Molly." Gertrude grinned.

"Humph!" said Molly. "I could have done without that."

Lucy laughed. "That's quite an honour. Just wait 'til I tell Larry."

"Tell Larry, indeed!" said Molly.

"He'll be jealous," said Lucy. "No one's ever named a dog after him, you know."

"By this time he should have a whole pack named after him," said Molly. "The way he neglected us on this case was shameful."

"We managed very nicely without him." Lucy preened herself a little. "Willie was quite determined to have his own way, especially when he didn't want to do something. It was a good experience."

"Humph!" said Molly. "I could have done without that particular experience."

"Now Molly, it wasn't his fault that his mother didn't love him. That'd be enough to warp anybody's personality."

"What did you two do to him up there, anyway?" asked Gertrude.

"Mostly sat on him," said Molly. "We realigned him and

reduced him to childhood, and generally kept him out of trouble. But mostly we sat on him."

"D'you mean literally sat on him? That must have been a picture."

"Sometimes," said Molly. "By the way, I understand that you're going into the baby business yourself quite soon."

"S-sh! Molly!" said Lucy. "You weren't supposed to tell her that."

"Well, I did," said Molly. "Anyway, it's time she knew."

"I am? Don will be so excited! I can't wait to tell him! See you later."

Molly turned to Lucy. "He won't be so happy when he finds out that his kid is psychic too."

Learn more about Margaret Westlie,
her life and her books, at
www.margaretwestlie.com.